HEART TAMER

SOPHIA KNIGHTLY

Alec and Kate – HEART TAMER
(Heartthrob Series, Novella)
Heart Tamer follows Heart Melter,
but can be read as a standalone

Kate Hayes has something she wants so desperately she's willing to swallow her pride and plead with her ex-husband, Alec MacLeod, for help. Up against a ticking clock, she must somehow convince him to go along with her unusual request. She and Alec parted on bad terms. Will he be able to put past hurt behind and embark on a life-changing journey?

Kate is the last person Alec expects—or wants—to see at his sister's wedding, but damn he's missed her. Her unforeseen arrival in Scotland makes him suspect she's up to something. Alec remembers why they parted and he's determined not to get pulled in, but seeing her again ignites a desire so intense he's tempted. Will he be able to resist? In this fiery second chance at love, whose heart will be tamed?

CHAPTER ONE

The ancient chapel door opened and gusts of icy Scottish air swept inside as the bagpipers quieted and the first chords of classical music drew the wedding guests to their feet. Kate shivered and hugged her gold velvet wrap tightly around her. It would take more than a wrap to warm her this late afternoon. Every nerve in her chilled body was leaping with anticipation…and anxiety.

Hunched behind an elegantly attired older couple, she was glad of the gap between their shoulders so she could peek behind the woman's fawn plumed hat at the wedding party without being noticed. Two stunning bridesmaids floated down the aisle in fuchsia satin gowns, one behind the other, then a pregnant redheaded matron of honor followed closely by an adorable dark-haired ring bearer and a little sprite of a blond flower girl.

The music segued into the glorious Canon in D Major wedding march. Any moment the bride would appear on her brother's arm. Her big brother who happened to be Kate's estranged ex-husband. She heaved a deep breath and willed the nervous jitters in her belly to stop wreaking havoc on her. She wasn't usually a nervous Nellie, but the stakes were high today. Too high for her to feel even remotely calm.

The moment Alec MacLeod's imposing form filled the entrance of the chapel, Kate almost lost her nerve. Almost...but not quite. She hadn't successfully raised rowdy twin brothers by being a wimp. So why was she wimping out now? Because her ex-husband was standing at the entrance of the church and he had no idea she was one of the guests. That was reason enough.

She uncurled from her crouched position and pushed her shoulders back in a stance that would have made late Aunt Loretta proud. But one glance at Alec entering with his younger sister, Eileen, on his arm and Kate couldn't contain the tears gathering in her eyes. The past years had been filled with sad events in their lives. Their youngest brother had died nine years ago and this year both of their parents had passed away, reducing the close knit family of five to two. It had to be a bittersweet moment for the close siblings as Alec stepped in for his father to give the bride away.

Kate could only imagine their pain, but she had never experienced that type of parental nurturing. Alec and Eileen had been raised by loving parents whereas Kate's parents had divorced shortly after her twin brothers were born. She was ten years old when her mom left her and the twins with Kate's elderly aunt one gray, winter night and never came back. Her shoulders drooped, but Aunt Loretta's stern voice rang in her ear. The memory of her aunt's voice chiding, *Katherine Hayes, do not slump like a schlump!* made her straighten right up.

In those days, she was always slumping. It was mortifying to have budding breasts when you were only ten. Even more mortifying to realize your mom and dad hadn't loved you enough to keep you. Kate's heart ached for her brothers especially. They didn't even know what their parents had looked like. When they were older and wanted details, Kate had told them the basics, leaving out heart-wrenching details of how her mother had remarried and raised her new husband's children as her own.

Kate shook off the bleak memories. Eileen's wedding was a joyous occasion, not a time for reflecting on the past. Giving into self-pity was useless and only made her feel worse. She couldn't change the past; she could only forge ahead with the present.

She gazed at Alec and her heart did crazy flip-flops at the mere sight of him. Dressed in formal Highland Scottish attire, his broad shoulders filled the black formal jacket to perfection. The green, turquoise and red MacLeod tartan kilt swathed his lean hips and was decorated by a silver dress sporran over his pelvis. She looked at Alec's brawny, muscular calves in tasseled wool knee socks and her knees turned to jelly remembering his massive strength tempered by incredible tenderness. When her gaze swept back up his 6'4" frame, she realized she was gaping like a fish. *Shut your mouth, you're drooling*, she chastised herself, dismayed by her show of weakness.

She forced her attention from Alec to gaze at Eileen fondly, thankful they'd remained friends after Kate's divorce. She was happy Eileen had found love and was embarking on a new life, one that would ease the pain of losing her parents. She'd been devastated by their untimely death and had told Kate she was glad to be moving to Edinburgh to begin a new life with Callum. The magnificent MacLeod family estate in Skye held too many poignant memories for Eileen to remain there. Eileen's radiant face glowed beneath the fingertip tulle veil and sparkling crystal and pearl tiara. Her upswept light brown curls showcased porcelain skin and wide amber eyes. The gown of ivory *peau de soie* and Belgian lace sheathed her slim torso in silk and flounced with yards and yards of Belgian lace from her tiny waist, adding curves to her otherwise boyish shape. Now a successful fashion designer in Manhattan, Kate had made the gown to Eileen's exact specifications. *I want to have an hourglass shape for once in my life, with hips and breasts—like yours,* she'd added eagerly, prompting an exaggerated eye roll from Kate. There was nothing boyish about Eileen tonight. With the plunging sweetheart neckline, she looked like a sexy, ethereal angel. Kate smiled and shook her head at the oxymoron.

The closer Alec got, the harder Kate's heart beat. She swallowed hard against a throat as dry as hay. The fine hairs on her arms prickled in anticipation of his reaction to seeing her at the wedding. She stood first in the third pew from the front and couldn't hide behind the elderly couple forever. She didn't want to either. The look on Alec's face when he saw her would be interesting…to say the least. Eileen hadn't told him Kate was invited or that she'd designed an exclusive bridal gown for her as a wedding gift. *Let him be surprised,* Eileen had said with a chuckle. It hadn't seemed amusing to Kate then and it certainly didn't now that Alec was getting closer.

By the time he reached her side, Kate's legs felt like liquid. Alec glanced at her and did a double take. Kate's hand flew to her chest as she sucked air into her suddenly constricted lungs. His dark gold leonine eyes narrowed beneath furrowed thick brows and flicked over her from head to toe. He gave her a curt nod. *That was it?* Alec's reaction utterly deflated her. He obviously thought she had no business being there. It cut her to the quick, but what had she expected? A welcoming smile? The warm twinkle in his eyes he'd once reserved for her?

She gave him a cautious smile, but his face had already turned impassive. With a set jaw and shuttered eyes, he turned his gaze away and escorted Eileen toward the altar.

Kate's heart squeezed, remembering the look of love in his eyes when he'd said, "I do" to her ten years ago. From the moment they'd met in a London pub, he lit her up like a firecracker and she'd never been the same since. Hot, astounding passion had reigned between them, robbing her of common sense. So much so that she did the only impulsive thing in her life—eloped with him only two months after they met, much to her Aunt Loretta's panic and the MacLeod family's surprised delight. She had been studying at the London College of Fashion and planning on returning to the States. But instead, she eloped and left everything behind to begin a new life in London as the wife of Alec MacLeod, a successful Scottish barrister practicing in London.

Everything should have gone well, but their passionate union was soon marred by bickering over things they should have discussed *before* getting married, like where they would live and if they wanted kids right away.

A year into the marriage, all communication spiraled downward when Alec's little brother Robbie tragically died. Alec became obsessed with tracking down the suppliers of tainted drugs that had killed Robbie at a college party. He shut out Kate and everyone close to him as he hunted down the drug dealers. Alec's emotional detachment eventually tore them apart as Kate felt lonely and terrified he would get killed while chasing down dangerous criminals. She reminded him she had married a lawyer not a detective, and she was alarmed he would end up dead like his brother Robbie.

After several months of living with limited communication, of agonizing each time he disappeared overnight to follow a lead, Kate issued an ultimatum— *stop putting yourself in danger or we get a divorce!* Alec had been so incensed when she'd threatened divorce that he walked out. And before she knew it, their marriage ended just as swiftly as it began. She had loved Alec more than she'd ever imagined possible and he blindsided her when he abruptly walked out.

Alec segued from being a barrister to owning a highly successful private security company in London. Eileen had told her he'd become a jaded ladies' man with no desire to remarry. It wasn't the best situation, but Kate would accept that—as long as he agreed to her plan. *Not bloody likely* as Alec often said, but definitely worth a try. She chewed her lower lip and stared at his broad shoulders where he sat in the front row rigid as a stone column, his head erect and wide shoulders squared. She was running out of time and she wouldn't give up her mission until he said yes. But she wasn't naïve enough to think he was any less stubborn than he'd been years ago.

Each had hot-blooded temperaments and were used to doing things their way. Alec's naturally dominant personality was often exasperated by her strong streak of independence. They were older now...and wiser. She could only hope that additional wisdom would help him keep an open mind.

She stared at the back of Alec's dark, wavy hair which grazed the collar of his white shirt. Most people considered him easy to get along with, but Kate wasn't most people. Alec had a highly developed analytical eye and keen curiosity. She knew him too well not to realize she'd aroused his suspicions.

What in bloody hell was she doing here? Just one glance at Kate and hot blood surged through Alec's body, muddling his senses with a flood of potent memories. He struggled to get a grip and concentrated on delivering his sister to Callum, who waited beside the priest with a beaming smile for his future bride.

With a heavy heart, Alec sat stoically in the first pew. The church was filled with family and loved ones, but the most important were missing—his parents and Robbie. He missed them profoundly…and he missed Kate, more than he wanted to admit. He hadn't been prepared for the gut clenching reaction he'd had when he locked eyes with her. First shock, then a desire so intense he almost lost his footing. Thanks to his career in global security he could blank out his reaction instantly and he'd drawn on that ability to the max just now.

He could feel Kate's presence behind him, but he doggedly kept his gaze from turning toward the third pew where she sat. Now that his wits were sharp again, it was all he could do not to snort like a bull. He shook his head at the irony. So Kate had crashed Eileen's wedding. Or had she? Glancing at Eileen's serene smile, Alec realized his ex-wife's attendance hadn't been a spur of the moment thing. Most likely, it had been planned by his meddling sister. He stifled a growl as he fingered the starched white collar of his dress shirt. His hands itched to wrap themselves around Eileen's sneaky neck and Kate's cheeky one.

Kate's glowing face played in his mind's eye. The moment their eyes met, she had looked vulnerable as bright pink flooded her face. She'd flashed a hesitant smile, but replaced it with a tautly pursed mouth when he gave her a dismissive nod. One look at her bristling green eyes and he knew her fiery temper was ignited. *Good, let her fume.* She was too bossy, opinionated and stubborn— all the things he'd overlooked when he'd married her because she was also generous, courageous and fun…and damned sexy.

Kate Hayes had made him lose his head enough to marry impulsively. He didn't have a rash bone in his body, except when it came to her and that's precisely why he'd kept away from her so long. When Kate threatened divorce, he thought she didn't love him as much as he loved her so he walked away before she did. Who knew how things would have turned out if it hadn't been for Robbie's death?

Kate might have been the one who got away, but had their marriage ever stood a chance after that first meeting at the pub? One look at her and he'd felt poleaxed. That had never happened with anyone. When she'd shared her past and told him how first her dad, then her mom had abandoned Kate and her twin brothers to be raised by an aunt, he had felt such an overwhelming urge to protect her, he couldn't let her go.

She was only 5'4" and he towered a foot above her when she was bare-footed, but her gutsy personality made up for her lack of height. He'd been completely intoxicated by her—her smile, her scent, her skin, her husky voice. The way her luscious curves filled his hands and her soft body molded to his *perfectly*. For two hedonistic months, they'd blocked the outside world and reveled in days and nights of carnal pleasure. After they eloped, they took a hasty trip to Scotland to meet his family, who adored her on the spot.

It wasn't until after they were married that Alec realized how obstinate she was. She was a real fighter when she wanted something. Smiling wryly, he remembered the only place he'd ever gotten her to surrender was in bed. What he'd give for a lusty weekend with her again. But he wasn't about to go there. Years ago when they'd left the divorce court, she had cried, *Hell will freeze over before I ever want to see you again!*

The feeling had been mutual. Kate was the last person he'd expected or had wanted to see today, but damn if she wasn't a sight for sore eyes.

CHAPTER TWO

Seated at an ivory and gold cloth-covered table with a cascading fuchsia rose centerpiece, Kate fidgeted and made polite small talk with a friendly couple named Don and Maisie. The other guests at the table were a newly married couple who couldn't stop cuddling and had no interest in socializing. Kate was the only singleton and the seat beside her was noticeably empty. The DJ was playing amazing music that made her want to dance, but she wasn't going to budge. It would be just her luck that the moment she left the table, Alec would finally show up.

She nibbled on the fig and goat cheese *tartine* and forced herself not to take another sweeping glance around the lavishly decorated hotel ballroom in search of her missing dinner companion. Eileen had arranged for Alec to sit beside Kate, but he was too busy socializing to eat. Going from table to table, greeting guests and giving the welcome toast, he hadn't sat down once. Nor had he given Kate another glance. Even when they'd processed out of the chapel, he'd kept his gaze away from hers. But all wasn't lost, she thought, watching Alec down a glass of champagne and clap a kilted friend on the back. His handsome friend with dark hair and light green eyes wore a different tartan, yet they were as comfortable as if they were brothers.

Go ahead, Alec, drink up and be merry. Mellow out before joining me at the table.

"Ah, there's Dr. MacGregor. He recently married an American actress named Natasha White. Do you know her?" Maisie asked Kate.

"Oh my God, yes. That's Natasha White. I knew I recognized her. I've seen her on Broadway!" Kate stared at the beautiful redheaded matron of honor leaning on Alec's friend's arm and laughing with them.

"They're expecting a bairn, and they adopted one too. That's him. Wee Arthur is dancing with the flower girl," Maisie nodded to the dance floor.

Kate followed her gaze and smiled, remembering how solemnly the ring bearer had walked up the aisle with the flower girl on his arm. The children were dancing as if they were contestants on a reality dance show. A pang of melancholy made her heart ache as she watched them dance. The baby she had lost in a miscarriage years ago would have had been a bit older than them.

Her pregnancy had come as a shock, but that hadn't lessened the devastating loss. She hadn't told Alec about it because she'd found out shortly after they had split up. He never knew about her miscarriage either. By then they'd grown even further apart. Everyone, especially Kate, had been shocked by the staggering speed of their divorce. It wasn't until two years later that she could talk about it without crying, especially since she'd lost Alec's baby too.

"Are you all right? You look upset." Maisie's worried tone snapped Kate back to the present.

"Yes, I'm fine." Kate made an effort to smile. "I didn't realize I looked sad. Could be watching the kids dance made me want to dance too," she said, feeling ridiculous at the lame excuse.

Maisie's blond brows drew together. "No need to feel sad. Don will dance with you, if you like."

"No thanks. Please don't ask him to," Kate said emphatically when Maisie turned to Don. "I really don't feel like dancing. Truth is, I was remembering how much my last boyfriend used to love to dance."

Small wonder Maisie gave her an odd look. She wasn't making any sense, but the last thing she wanted was a pity dance with Maisie's husband whom she had just met. She gulped down the rest of her wine. "That little boy is so cute. I love the way he twirls her around."

"Wee Arthur was one of Dr. MacGregor's patients before he and Natasha adopted him." Maisie's cheeks puffed up proudly. "One side of the lad's face used to be covered by a purple mark. The mark is much smaller now because of Dr. MacGregor's laser work. Soon it will be completely gone. That's what I've heard."

Kate nodded. "It's amazing what lasers can do these days. Eileen told me about Dr. MacGregor's clinic. She's excited about working there."

"How do you know Eileen?" Maisie wasn't wearing make-up and she didn't need any. Her lips were ruby red and her fair cheeks tinged scarlet from an abundance of the cabernet sauvignon wine. She ran a hand over her updo of a tumble of blond curls and smiled at Kate, waiting for her answer.

"We've been friends for years," Kate finally said, choosing not to elaborate. She couldn't exactly say, "I'm Alec's ex-wife" without opening a can of worms.

"You're American, aren't you?" Maisie's bright blue eyes studied Kate with curiosity. She must have seen Alec's name tag beside Kate's place and was probably dying to ask more, but so far she hadn't mentioned Alec.

"Yes. I'm a New Yorker." Good thing Maisie and her husband Don were friendly and keeping her company, otherwise she'd be sitting there like a wallflower. The newlyweds had left and were entwined on the dance floor swaying to a slow song.

Don inclined his head politely. "New York is a fine city. Maisie and I visited last year during Christmas. What do you do there?"

Kate smiled. "I'm a fashion designer."

Maisie's eyes widened with delight. "A fashion designer! Lovely. Did you make clothes for your dolls as a little girl?"

Kate smiled at the image. Her childhood had been the antithesis of playing with dolls. She'd had to balance going to school, raising her twin brothers and working for Miss Claire, the fanciful seamstress who made exclusive bridal gowns in Brooklyn. Aunt Loretta had had a kind heart beneath her stern personality, but she had been a penny-pinching tightwad and Kate had wanted to give her brothers the things other little boys had at their age. It wasn't their fault their parents had abandoned them. She'd been determined to give Ryan and Reed as normal a childhood as possible to make up for it. She'd worked after school and many evenings doing sewing alterations to pay for the extras Aunt Loretta deemed a frivolous waste.

"Did you design the gown you're wearing? I love that vibrant shade of green. What is your label name?" Maisie asked.

"Kate Couture." After Aunt Loretta died, Kate and her brothers inherited a hefty amount. Kate had been astounded by how much money her aunt had had in her savings, especially since she'd lived so frugally. Her inheritance had funded a one-bedroom apartment in Manhattan and Kate's investment in a partnership with Evangeline, her best friend from design school. They were part owners of the exclusive bridal boutique, Kate and Evie, in the Upper East Side.

"Are you friends of the bride or groom?" Kate said, turning the subject away from her.

"The groom," Maisie and Don replied in unison. "We've known Callum since he was a wee bairn."

From the corner of her eye, Kate watched Alec draw a sexy brunette onto the dance floor. She forced herself not to stare at them and concentrated on listening to Maisie as she told her what a great kid Callum had been growing up. Kate smiled politely and hoped she didn't look as pitiful as she felt, ignored and rejected by Alec.

She barely noticed when a server removed the appetizer and placed a plate of roast lamb chops, herbed red potatoes with fennel, green peas and baby carrots before her. Alec was dancing with another girl now. Well, at least it was a different girl. Eileen had assured her he didn't have a girlfriend. Not that it made a difference to her, but it would complicate her plan.

She had spent a fun Christmas week with her younger brothers, Reed and Ryan, skiing in Vermont before leaving for the wedding. With the peace of mind that they were both doing well in grad school, Kate could get started on her new life goal as soon as possible. All Christmas long, she'd prayed for only one thing for the New Year and if all went well, her fondest wish would come true in Scotland.

Kate watched Eileen and Callum cut the three-tiered butter cream frosted cake and feed each other to the many toasts and blessings the wedding party bestowed on them.

"Just a few hours till midnight now. Have you ever spent Hogmanay in Edinburgh?" Don asked.

"No, but I hear it's quite a celebration." Kate sank her fork into the wedding cake and nearly swooned when she tasted it. Her ardent sweet tooth welcomed the luscious raspberry mousse and plump, fresh raspberries nestled between the layers of fluffy vanilla cake. The best part of the wonderful meal was the cake. It kept her from dousing her growing ire over Alec's rude dismissal with wine and champagne.

"Aye, a celebration that lasts into the wee hours of the morning." Maisie's eyes flashed with excitement. "In Edinburgh, there are fireworks and much partying around the castle. Every region has different customs, but we always gather together to sing *Auld Lang Syne* with our arms linked together as the clock strikes midnight."

"Sounds wonderful," Kate said absently, wishing she could summon Maisie's enthusiasm. The longer the evening progressed without Alec's presence, the more pessimistic she felt.

A cool hand touched Kate's shoulder making her turn so quickly, she dropped her fork.

"Sorry I startled you, Kate," Eileen said, laughing softly. "Callum and I wanted to thank you for coming all the way from America to celebrate with us."

"Are you kidding? I wouldn't miss it for the world." Kate rose from the table and hugged Eileen tightly. She released her and hugged Callum next, pulling back to smile into his twinkling brown eyes. It was her first time meeting him, and she liked him instantly. It was obvious he was mad about Eileen, and Eileen had never been this happy in love. "Congratulations, you two! What a beautiful wedding! Everything is perfect and the food is delicious."

"I'm glad." Eileen smiled. "I know I've told you a thousand times already, but I *love* this gown so much. Thank you for designing it for me."

"You're very welcome," Kate said. "You look stunning in it."

"*You* designed her gown?" Maisie's blue eyes popped open. "It's gorgeous and you're gorgeous in it, Eileen!" She and Don sprang from their seats and they took turns hugging Eileen and Callum heartily.

"Congratulations! May you have many, many years of love and happiness like Maisie and me," Don said, beaming at them.

Eileen thanked them and then stared at the empty chair beside Kate with a furrowed brow. "Has Alec come by yet?" she asked Kate in a low voice as Callum chatted with Maisie and Don.

"Nope, and from the looks of it, he might never," Kate said, trying to keep the disappointment from her voice. She motioned with her chin across the room where Alec was seated at a table flanked by two smiling bridesmaids.

Eileen followed her gaze and shook her head as her eyes clouded with displeasure. "Excuse me. I'll be right back," she said before Kate could stop her.

When the sexy brunette Alec had been dancing with earlier came up to chat with him, the two bridesmaids got up and headed to the bar. Kate pasted a polite smile on her face and headed there too. She was tired of sitting at the table while everyone, especially Alec, was living it up on the dance floor. Out of the corner of her eye, she saw him go back to the dance floor with Sexy Brunette.

Kate stood at the bar next to the two beautiful bridesmaids who held martinis and chatted like best friends. Both seemed to be in their early twenties with long brown hair in spiral curls. Their fuchsia dresses highlighted their slim figures and porcelain skin.

Kate smiled at the bartender. "I'll have a club soda and cranberry juice please." Her ears immediately perked up when one of the bridesmaids said, "Becky, look at Sheena. Do you believe how cheeky she is? She's been chasing Mr. Yumminess all night."

"Big surprise. She's always had a thing for him. But Alec's the love 'em and leave 'em type. He'll spend the night with her and then leave first thing in the morning, like he always does," Becky said resignedly. "Right, Justine?"

"Don't ask me. How would I know?" Justine grinned. "Anyway…a girl can always dream. Alec is wicked hot, but he's always up front about not wanting to get married again." She rolled her eyes. "Sheena knows that, but she thinks she can change him."

"Maybe she will. Look at them," Becky said, nudging her.

"I don't want to. Let's go back. She's monopolizing Alec's time." Justine grabbed Becky's arm and drinks in hand, they headed toward the table.

Kate set her glass down and made a beeline to the ladies' room for immediate strategizing. The moment she entered the ladies' room, her throat clogged and her eyes welled up. *This is ridiculous.* She angrily swiped at her eyes, surprised by her extreme sappiness tonight. She felt humiliated that Alec was publicly dissing her with Sheena. Most of the guests didn't even realize it, so why should she feel so rejected? And why should she be so surprised? It wasn't as if they'd parted on good terms and kept in touch.

Her friendship with Eileen had strengthened over the years, but she hadn't seen or spoken to Alec since their divorce. Small surprise he was avoiding her. Still, it rankled that he'd be so dismissive. Couldn't he be gracious? Eileen had told her Alec dated a lot, so she wasn't surprised he was popular with the ladies tonight. But she hadn't counted on Sheena...

Growing more annoyed by the minute, Kate blew her nose furiously. If Alec wasn't capable of coming to her, she'd go to him. Since when had she let his mulishness stop her? *Since the divorce...* Well, things were different now and she hadn't come all the way to Scotland to cower in the ladies' room. She was there to get what she wanted, even if it meant chasing after it.

Kate flung the door open and headed to the grand ballroom where Alec was groovin' to the music with Sheena. She had long, straight black hair parted in the middle, and she wore a burnished silver mini dress that cupped her perky behind. Swaying sensuously to the music, she flung her hair from side to side and sent smoky-eyed glances toward Alec, who was holding his own on the dance floor. Despite his large stature and muscular physique, he was light on his feet and moved with incredible rhythm.

Kate walked up to them as soon as the music stopped. "Excuse me please. I need to talk to Alec. It's urgent." Sheena ignored Kate and looked at Alec, waiting for his reaction.

Alec exhaled a heavy sigh. "It seems Kate and I need to have a wee chat. You'll save another dance for me, won't you, Sheena?"

"Aye," Sheena said reluctantly, giving Kate the evil eye. She squeezed Alec's hand and smoldered at him from beneath long lashes. "Later," she promised before tossing her sleek hair over one shoulder and leaving.

The grooves beside Alec's mouth deepened into slashes and his tawny eyes studied Kate from beneath knitted brows. "So, Katie, has hell frozen over then?"

Alec's sardonic question annoyed her and the fact that he brought up the last thing she had said to him after their divorce irked her even more.

"Were you planning on ignoring me all night?" she asked with a thrust of her chin. Good thing she was wearing stiletto heels and didn't have to crane her head too far back to look at him. With that jab, he didn't deserve one inch, let alone twelve inches of advantage over her.

"You're hard to ignore. I recognize that look on your face. What do you want?" Alec's question rolled off his tongue with a deep Scots burr, sending a shiver of apprehension through her. He was no slouch as an interrogator. She'd have to keep her cool so they could come to a compromise. *Even if she had to be the lamb to his wolf.*

"No need to be suspicious," she murmured lightly. She held out her hand. "Shall we dance?"

"Aye. Why not?" Alec said, more to himself than to Kate. His large hand closed over her hand as his other warm hand settled on the small of her back. A shockwave of sensations skittered up her spine as he pulled her toward him, leaving no doubt who was leading whom.

CHAPTER THREE

Kate wished they were anywhere but on the dance floor. But what else could she do? She'd had to move quickly when she saw how Sheena was coming on to Alec. If she hadn't, it would only be a matter of time before Alec and Sheena headed out together.

As they danced, Alec's lean hips moved in a sensual, leisurely way that drew Kate's immediate attention. Her stomach fluttered as she thought of what lay beneath the sporran covering his pelvis. One glance at him and she caught his raised eyebrow. Damn him, he always seemed to know what she was thinking.

"Why the change of heart?" she said when the music slowed down.

"What do you mean?" It was hard to overlook his palm pressed firmly on her lower back, the fingertips hovering above the top swell of her bottom. In the past, that hand wouldn't have remained still. It would have roamed the round contours of her buttocks, stroking and squeezing to his heart's content. His other hand enveloped hers, strong and assured, with tapered fingers she knew were adept at creating magic. At the moment, the slight pressure of those very fingers was wreaking havoc on her composure.

She drew in a steadying breath. It was the first time they'd been so physically close in a long while and she wasn't prepared for the onslaught of heady sensations and emotions. Heat flooded every pore of her wobbly body as she tried to maintain a semblance of poise.

"First you glare at me at church, then you ignore me all evening and now you're dancing with me."

"I didn't glare at you. I was surprised to see you, verra surprised. Curious too." Alec pulled her closer and his mouth hovered at her temple. "Eileen didn't tell me you'd be here," he said in a low voice, his warm breath tickling her ear.

Gooseflesh spread over her bare arms and she dearly hoped he didn't notice. "She didn't? And here I wondered why you'd requested to sit by me and never showed up."

"You'll have to do better than that, wee Katie. What prompted you to show up here after so many years?"

"I came for the wedding. And don't call me wee Katie."

"You haven't told me *why* you came."

She stiffened. "My friendship with your sister didn't end with our divorce. It's no surprise she would invite me to her wedding."

"Aye, but that doesn't explain why Eileen kept it a secret."

"I asked her not to tell you I was coming."

"You shouldn't have done that." His gruff tone said he didn't like them keeping a secret from him.

"I wanted a chance to talk to you...to discuss something very important."

He slowed down and leaned back to study her face. "Oh? And what would that be?"

Alec's tawny eyes penetrated hers, but she couldn't divulge the real purpose of her trip in the middle of a dance floor. He might stalk away and then she'd have to follow him. They needed to speak in private, but after the way they had ended it all those years ago, he probably wouldn't agree. Their fights had been too passionate...their tempers too hot. They'd had a constant a battle of wills that sometimes escalated into passionate fights and ended with Alec's erotic lovemaking. She shivered at the toe-curling memories.

"It's something mutually beneficial." *Good,* she had Alec's full attention now, and it was time to go in for the kill. With a slight shimmy of her shoulders, Kate inched closer, the tips of her breasts brushing against the lapels of his wool jacket. "Keep an open mind and maybe we can cut a deal," she said with a cryptic smile, enjoying how his eyes lit up.

Alec stopped dancing and stared at Kate. What game was she playing? He couldn't take one more second of her breasts barely touching him. If she moved in any closer, his physical response would be hard to hide. Pulling back to gaze at her hadn't helped either. Kate's luscious body was draped in a jaw-dropping strapless jade dress that emphasized full, round breasts, a small waist and shapely hips. What was he thinking dancing with her? He was already hard as a poker. *Damn fool!* Too many cups of wine and he'd already succumbed to temptation in the form of wee Katie and her dangerous curves.

He shook his head and considered what she had just said. *Maybe we can cut a deal.* What kind of deal? Bloody hell, it was all he could do not to drag her from the dance floor to find out.

"This isn't the place for a private conversation." He lightly clasped her above the elbow and led her away.

"Hey, slow down. I can't keep up with you." Kate's high heels clicked on the marble floor as she tried to keep up with his long strides.

"What are you doing in those ridiculously high stilettos?" he muttered even though he knew why she'd worn them. Not one to be bested by his height, Kate had made damn sure she would be as close to eye level as possible.

Alec released her arm when they reached the lobby. The feel of her soft skin was distracting and he needed a clear head to deal with her. He came to a halt before two antique chairs and an ornate Victorian sofa.

With his hands on his hips, he leaned in close. "Okay, out with it."

Kate shook her head. "Not here. It's not a good place to talk. Too many people milling around." She gestured toward a group getting off the elevator and heading toward them.

He clasped her upper arm again. "Then we'll go outside."

She arched an eyebrow and stared at his hand encircling her arm until he released it.

"It's too cold out there and I left my wrap at the table. Can't we find someplace a little more...secluded?" She paused and smiled, a slight catlike lift of her lips. A smile of seduction. *Interesting... Two* could play this game.

"Then we'll go to my room."

"Your room?"

"Aye. We'll have that chat you're set on having."

She stepped up to him so close he got a tantalizing whiff of flowers. His gaze dipped to her soft, bare nape above the coppery, chestnut hair swept back in a loose updo. He wanted to release the pins and run his fingers through her glossy hair, to unzip her dress and bury his face in her pillowy, fragrant breasts...

"What about the guests?" she asked, interrupting his fantasies.

"The party's almost over. They won't notice we're gone. Let's go."

Alec watched her bravado slip as she stood before him, wide green eyes vulnerable and lips slightly parted. All playfulness vanished as she swallowed visibly and nodded.

Alec's suite was simply magnificent. Kate glanced around the spacious room, awed by its sumptuous décor from the gleaming mahogany antiques to the marble fireplace before the pearl gray sofa. In her thriving business, she was invited to many destination weddings and often stayed in hotel rooms, but this one surpassed them all. For a girl who'd grown up having to share a room with boisterous twin brothers, spending a night on luxury sheets and ordering room service was her idea of sheer heaven.

The first time she'd ever spent the night in a hotel suite was on her honeymoon with Alec. She remembered the dizzying excitement as if it were yesterday. And from the smoldering look in Alec's heavy-lidded eyes, he was remembering it too.

"Let's sit by the fire," Alec said, his voice huskier than usual.

Kate perched on the edge of the sofa while he crossed to the sideboard.

"Would you like a drink?" he asked.

"No, thanks." She needed to keep her wits sharp around him.

Alec seemed to be in no hurry as he took off his jacket and sporran and laid them over a chair. He untied the black cravat and loosened the collar of his shirt, then rolled up his sleeves revealing muscular, brown forearms. She'd always found his swarthy skin appealing. The contrast with his topaz eyes and dazzling white smile made his rugged face all the more enticing. He stretched his arms out and rolled his neck from side to side before pouring scotch into a cut crystal glass.

If he was getting comfortable, she might as well too. Kate slipped out of her shoes and massaged her aching feet as she sat back on the sofa and replayed the reason she was here. Eileen had confided many things, but what bolstered her most was hearing her say, *Alec would never admit it, but he's lonely. All his friends are married, and most have children. Now I'm getting married too. He has a lot of women, but he hasn't had a relationship with any of them...since you.* Eyeing how hot he looked, she wondered if Eileen had exaggerated just to get them back together again.

He was already drawing her to him like a hypnotist. She couldn't afford a replay of the past where a meaningful look from him was all it took to land her in bed for steamy, heart-throbbing, knee-melting sex. The bridesmaid at the bar had said Alec was the love 'em and leave 'em type. If had been capable of leaving Kate once, he'd do it again. She couldn't bear to feel that broken again.

By the time Alec joined her on the sofa, Kate's nerves were bouncing like popcorn kernels in a sizzling pan. He took a long swig of scotch, set the glass on the coffee table and turned his full attention on her. Up close, his eyes were the color of golden sherry with chocolate colored flecks. Surrounded by lush, dark lashes, those gleaming eyes alone would tempt a saint. She scooted over. Alec was a large man and she didn't want to be distracted by his knee, or any part of him, touching her.

"So…how have you been, Katie?" His eyes explored her face with a mixture of curiosity and something akin to fondness. It took her by surprise. She had expected him to be impatient to know what she wanted, but he seemed genuinely interested in knowing how she was doing. The constricted feeling in her chest eased up a bit.

"I'm fine." She paused and collected her thoughts, which wasn't easy with him looking at her that way. "Business is great. I own a bridal boutique with my partner, Evangeline. It's called Kate and Evie." She smiled. "We work hard, but I can't complain."

He nodded. "Good to hear. How are the boys doing?"

A fuzzy feeling tickled her belly as she gazed at him appreciatively. It meant a lot to her that he'd asked about her brothers. "Ryan is getting his M.B.A and Reed is in law school. I'm very proud of how hard they've worked." She wanted to say much more, but it was impossible to condense ten years in a brief conversation. Instead she said, "Alec, I never got to tell you how sorry I was to hear of your parents' passing. They were wonderful people." She paused and swallowed as her throat thickened with sadness. "And I loved them."

Alec scrubbed a weary hand over his eyes. His eyes suddenly looked bloodshot and his face was set in somber lines. "Aye. It's been a sad year. I miss them very much. Granny Bessie passed a few months ago too."

Eileen had told her how Alec had stayed by his dying granny's side in hospice the final days before she died. His compassion for his elderly grandma had touched Kate deeply. Underneath the big, tough man lurked a marshmallow heart. He was the kindest man she knew— when he wasn't being mule-headed.

"I'm sorry about her passing. Your granny was such fun. I remember her naughty jokes and twinkling eyes."

Alec smiled warmly. "Aye, her naughty humor was too funny," he said, shaking his head. His eyes grew earnest as he leaned forward, elbows on his knees. "It was tough to see how she deteriorated at the end. After Mum died, Granny shut down, emotionally and physically."

Kate could only imagine how desperate he'd felt, wanting to do more for his granny and incapable of easing her suffering. "That must have been hard on you and Eileen. How are you doing now?" she said, searching his solemn face.

"Life goes on and we have to make the best of what we have," he said quietly. "I have big decisions to make. Whether to keep the MacLeod family estate or sell it. Eileen wants me to sell. She says being there makes her miss Mum and Dad too much. It could be because their passing is so recent. I don't want to make a rash decision, but I need to return to London soon. I have a good life there."

"Oh," she said, feeling a bit dejected. What else had she expected? Of course he had a good life. Alec was an extrovert. He had a ton of friends...especially lady friends.

Kate looked down at her hands and sighed. It was now or never. She couldn't sit there all evening dithering over how she was going to ask him a crucial, life-changing question. *Time to suck it up, buttercup!* That was Evie's favorite saying and today it really fit the bill.

"Katie?" The question in Alec's voice nudged her into action.

She lifted her face and met his penetrating gaze with a lift of her brows.

"What's this about? As I recall, you mentioned cutting a deal," he said dryly.

Was that a twinkle in his eyes? Had to be the whiskey that was making him mellow.

"Oh...ha! Well, that was a bit of an exaggeration. I'm here because I want—" She stopped abruptly. *Nooo, don't begin with "I want", dummy!* It was too self-serving, even though this visit was all about what she wanted more than anything in the world.

She got progressively anxious as she struggled to find the right words. A fine mist of cold sweat covered her skin as she clenched her hands into a tight knot on her lap so he wouldn't see them trembling. She gulped in air and exhaled it slowly, wilting under his probing gaze.

"Are you okay? You look like you're about to pass out." He rose from the sofa. "Maybe you should have a wee drink."

Kate reached up to detain him. The moment she touched Alec's hard forearm, she snatched it back. She wasn't there to be seduced by his muscles. She had a mission and needed to see it through without caving to his manly appeal. It alarmed her how the mere touch of his skin and the feel of his controlled strength made her senses reel with longing.

"No drink. I'm fine. Really," she added when he gave her a disbelieving look. "I'm just a bit nervous that's all." She looked down at her clenched hands and unclenched them. There was no need to act as if she were going to a death chamber. The worse that could happen is he'd get annoyed and say no. She didn't want to consider the Pandora's box she'd be opening with one simple request. It wasn't really simple though…it was life changing—for both of them.

Alec sat down again and took her frozen hand in his. The warmth of his touch gave her courage. "Don't be nervous. Tell me what you want."

"It's a bit unusual," Kate hedged.

His dark brows lifted. "What is it?"

She had rehearsed this moment a million times, preparing a speech worthy of an Oscar. But all she could do was stare at him, panic-stricken. What was she doing here, putting her heart on the line? And what made her think he'd be any different now. In the past, their fights had been because he claimed she was too bossy, when in reality he was a major alpha male. Her problem, which she freely admitted to herself only—was too much pride and the fear of losing face. She'd been working on it for years. This was the ultimate test. Would she be able to swallow her pride and risk losing face?

"Well?" he prodded, tilting her chin to gaze directly into her eyes.

She lowered her gaze from his and said a quick prayer for strength. She could feel his mystified eyes on her as she looked down and considered the outcome if she didn't speak up now. She inhaled deeply, drew on the pluck that had gotten her to this point in her life and decided she'd rather sacrifice her pride than risk losing what she wanted most in life.

Kate lifted one shoulder in a half-shrug and gave Alec a wobbly smile. "I want to have your baby."

CHAPTER FOUR

Alec shot up from the couch as if someone had jabbed him with a long needle. He waved his hand at her lap and then to the front of his kilt with a look of utter shock. "You and me? Have a bairn?" Standing wide-legged with his fists planted on his hips, he stared at her as if she'd lost her mind. "Never in a million years did I imagine you'd come all the way over to proposition me."

Kate's face blazed. "Knock it off. I'm not propositioning you. I said I wanted to have your baby, not have sex with you."

"Last time I checked the way you have a bairn is through sex. Fucking to be exact," he said bluntly. "Marriage is usually in order too."

"Who said anything about marriage?" She stood up and faced him squarely. "This has nothing to do with marriage or making love. I have something else in mind."

He snorted. "This I want to hear."

She couldn't get into details just yet. Not with that ornery look on his face. No need to wave a red cape in front of the bull. "I'm not asking you to marry me or anything like that. If we have a baby together, I'll take care of raising him or her. You don't even have to be involved, though I think it's good for a baby to have a father if possible."

"Damn right it is." He watched her through narrowed eyes. "It's been years. Why now? Why me?"

Kate couldn't exactly say, *Because I've never forgotten the baby we lost. I never loved anyone as much as I loved you, and if I can't have you, I want your baby.* Her heart raced like a wild filly as she debated what to say. She went for the obvious. "You have so many qualities that I would want my baby to have."

Alec's distrustful topaz eyes didn't waver from Kate's. "Like what?"

She smiled wryly. "Now you're fishing for compliments. Okay, well, to begin with you're very smart, strong and a born leader. You have an abundance of kindness and you're an extrovert. You genuinely like people and they like you. Those are traits I'd love for my baby to have."

"Thanks." He eyed her with interest. "But I still don't understand what brought this on. The last I saw of you, you were screeching you never wanted to see me again."

"I don't screech," she huffed. "Anyway, what did you expect after a divorce? Compliments?"

He scoffed. "Hardly."

Kate shrugged. "I've matured and I know what I want out of life now. I spent my youth raising my brothers and working hard. After our divorce, I threw myself into building a business that I loved so I could be independent and support myself."

"I offered to pay you a generous alimony, but you refused," he reminded her with a grim set of his jaw.

"I didn't want your money." *I wanted you!* she silently shouted. "I never expected you to walk out on me and I vowed I'd never depend on a man again to support me or to make me happy."

"Good for you," he said with a hint of sarcasm. "You're independent and you don't need anyone."

"I didn't say that. I do need someone. A baby." Her eyes met his earnestly. "Not just any baby. I want your baby," she said with more bravado than she felt.

"I'm not planning on getting married again," he said brusquely.

"I already told you I'm not asking you to marry me," she said, exasperated he was fixating on that.

Alec's dark brows knotted over puzzled eyes, steadily watching her as if he just couldn't grasp her motives. "So you keep insisting, but most women expect it."

"I'm not like most women," she said with a lift of her chin.

"Aye, that's for sure," he said readily. He gave a slow shake of his head. "Why would I agree to this?"

"Don't you want a child? Someone to call your own and carry on your clan's name? That's important in Scotland. Isn't it?"

He lifted a single brow and smirked. "Cut the bullshit, Katie. You don't give a damn about our Scottish traditions."

"That's not true. Whatever gave you that idea? I love Scottish traditions," she said, wounded. "My most treasured memories are the times I spent in Skye with your parents."

Alec exhaled a heavy sigh and rubbed the back of his neck. "Why would I agree to bring a wee child into this world without two loving parents to raise it? Life is hard enough."

At this point she was desperate. At her last exam, Dr. Healey had told her if she wanted a baby, she needed to try as soon as possible, or she might not be able to conceive. "Do it for the memory of your parents. They so wanted us to have children."

A shadow of pain crossed his face. "That's not fair, Katie. Mum and Dad wanted grandchildren badly because they lost Robbie. You must have known that."

Kate's heart sank. Alec looked stricken. She wished she hadn't brought up the painful past. "Yes, I'm sorry. I didn't mean to dredge up Robbie's death."

Alec's eyes clouded at the devastating memory. "When Robbie died, I felt helpless and sick with rage at the injustice." His fists clenched at his sides. "I couldn't bring him back, but I sure as hell could avenge his death by putting the culprits in jail. You never understood how badly I needed to make things right by Robbie."

Kate laid a gentle hand on his shoulder. "I'm sorry. I should have been more understanding, more accommodating."

Alec nodded. "Aye."

"But I wasn't the only one at fault. You knew I was terrified you'd end up like Robbie, yet you persisted in putting your life in danger while you went after the drug dealers. I couldn't bear the thought of losing you. I had already lost both my parents and I'm not good at losing someone I love." She looked skyward and shook her head. "Talking about this makes me feel worse. Ironically, I lost you anyway."

"It was a bad parting. Not something I'm proud of." He gave a rueful shake of his head. "I'm surprised you're here now, wanting to have my bairn. But when you get something in your head, there's no stopping you."

She drew in a shaky breath as her eyes beseeched him. "So...will you do it?"

Alec's mood seemed to lift as he gazed at her in bemusement. His discerning eyes swept over her, taking in every inch of her body. The moments ticked by with agonizing slowness. She began to feel nauseated and sick at heart that he'd say no.

He finally gave a casual shrug. "Sure."

"You will?" Kate staggered backward and reached for his arms to steady herself. She was floored he'd agreed so readily. Alec wasn't a man to be easily led about.

"Aye. Why not? It will be nice to reconnect with your sweet body, lass," he said with a slow smile

"Hold on. Who said anything about my sweet body? I don't mean to be crass, but I only want your sperm." She ignored his affronted look and continued briskly, "I have a document in my room I'll bring over for you to sign."

"What does it say?" His voice was brusque and dangerously low.

"It's an agreement that you will donate your sperm to me with no strings attached. I'll take care of everything else."

"Is that so?" he asked in a deceptively calm voice.

"Yes," she mumbled, realizing how demanding and unreasonable it sounded when she said it out loud. But what else could she do? Alec didn't love her anymore. She couldn't have sex with him without his love. It would break her heart. But she wanted his baby so badly she was willing to do anything to get it. She might have lost Alec's love, but she would always have his child's love.

Alec sprawled on the sofa and took hold of her wrist. With a firm pull, he settled her on his lap. "Don't waste your time, lass. I won't sign it."

"Why not?" she demanded, wriggling to escape his hard thighs.

Alec's hand formed a steely handcuff around her wrist. "Stop wiggling about. Your arse feels so round and soft, we'll end up conceiving that bairn right here," he growled.

"No, we won't. Let go of me," she snapped, even though the feel of his stiff arousal made her squeeze her thighs against a gush of excitement.

He took her chin in his hand and turned her face toward him. "If you want to have my bairn that badly, wee Katie, we'll conceive it the natural way." He gave a meaningful pause. "I'll have your sweet surrender."

Open-mouthed, Kate stared at him. The silence between them grew and tension mounted as seconds ticked by.

The corners of Alec's mouth lifted into a sardonic smile. His glittering eyes locked on hers, forcing her to hold his gaze. "And you'll have to ask for it nicely...*verra nicely*." He patted her bottom. "I'm in charge now."

CHAPTER FIVE

Talk about infuriating! Kate couldn't believe Alec was toying with her when she had just bared her soul to him. She felt like smacking him.

"Sorry to disappoint you, but I'm not here to inflate your already enormous ego. I'm not going to beg either, no matter how much I want your baby." Begging a man to stay didn't work. She was only eight when she saw her very pregnant mother on her knees shaking, crying and begging for Kate's dad not to leave them, yet he'd callously walked out. That sickening image haunted Kate to this day.

He slid her off his lap onto the space beside him and brushed his hands together as if saying good riddance. "Did you think I'd agree to have a baby because you asked for it? I was just testing you to see how far you would go to get your way."

"Testing me? How dare you." Hot fury made her temples pound. "Forget I even asked. I don't want you to be the father any more. I'll go to a sperm bank!"

"You'll do no such thing," Alec muttered edgily.

"I'll do *exactly* what I want. Nobody tells me what to do. Contrary to what you think, Mr. Big Ego, you are not in charge! By next year I'll be pregnant," Kate vowed, dearly hoping she was right. She shoved her feet in her shoes and bolted up from the sofa. With her head held high and a rigid backbone, she stalked away.

"Where are you going?" he demanded, following closely behind.

"I'm going to dance and have a good time. There were lots of good-looking guys out there and I'm planning on enjoying the party. Who knows, maybe I'll get lucky tonight and meet someone—"

"Over my dead body." Alec glared at her through narrowed dark gold eyes as he took hold of her wrist.

"Start planning your funeral then," she said, shaking off his grip. "Before I go, I'll have that drink you offered." She walked to the bar, poured two inches of scotch and knocked down the liquor, choking and wheezing as it scalded her poor esophagus.

Alec's caustic chuckle followed her coughing fit. "Still a lightweight, eh Katie?"

His smug observation was the last straw. It was a miracle steam didn't blow out of her ears. Her hand trembled on the bottleneck as she poured another two inches of scotch. Holding his gaze, she downed the contents and this time made sure not to utter a peep, even though her insides were blazing with reproach. Kate opened her mouth to say something, but the raw feeling in her throat made her snap it shut. The last thing she wanted was to croak like a frog.

"Slow down. Scotch shouldn't be wasted on those who can't handle it."

Was he trying to make her see red? Kate's temper was already teetering on a fine line between control and explosion.

He took the bottle from her hands. "Give me that. I don't want to have to carry you to your room."

"You wish! You won't be touching one inch of me tonight. Get out of my way," Kate shouted, hopping mad.

Alec blocked the door, his eyes stony and mouth set. "Lower your voice. You haven't changed a bit. Still bossy and damned stubborn."

"Stop flapping your mouth and move out of my way. If you think I'm going to stand here one more second and—" The rest of her words were muffled as Alec pulled her to him and kissed her hard, his arms anchored around her back.

"Shut up." His mouth ground against hers as his hands slid down and cupped her bottom, lifting her upward. Her shoes fell to the floor as she dangled in the air. Bracing her hands on his rock hard biceps she tried to protest, to insist that he stop kissing her, but her body's instant, wild response betrayed her. She opened her lips and allowed his tongue to glide inside. The moment he began to ravenously taste her, all resistance melted and gave way to fierce desire.

Alec's kisses were carnal and deep and his erection thick, leaving no doubt where they were headed. He carried her toward the bedroom, kicked the door open and tumbled onto the bed with her. He hiked her gown up to her waist and braced himself on his elbows above her, holding his weight from crushing her.

Lowering her strapless bustier to free her breasts, he lifted them in his large hands. She inhaled sharply when his dark head bent and his mouth nuzzled her nipples.

They tightened pleasurably beneath the whoosh of his warm breath and the velvety softness of his lips. The pad of his tongue lightly flicked the taut tips before sucking deeply, causing a yearning so intense Kate gasped. "So beautiful," he murmured gutturally.

Hot, wet desire pooled between her trembling thighs as his mouth traveled up her neck and kissed the soft spot behind her ear leaving a trail of gooseflesh everywhere his lips touched. Her pulse throbbed wildly as his bold fingers dipped into her panties and skillfully stroked her slick arousal. She moaned deep in her throat at the thrilling, intimate exploration.

Kate's lower belly quivered with erotic spasms and her legs felt like jelly as she squirmed and gripped his forearms. Squeezing her eyes shut, she drew in shallow breaths and tried to hold on to the last shred of control. But she was close...alarmingly close to the mind-blowing *sweet surrender* he'd asked for earlier. Acute, pleasurable sensations formed a spiraling tornado that spread from the apex of her swollen sex to every tingling nerve ending of her body.

Alec's fingers stopped abruptly and pulled back to look at her. The gleaming ferocity in his eyes took her breath away.

"No. Don't stop!" she said, practically hyperventilating.

"What do you want, Katie?" he gritted in a taut voice.

"I want *you,* Alec."

He peeled her panties down and off. "I want to see you shatter in my arms...to be the one who makes you lose control."

"Yes," she panted, her voice throaty as air barely escaped her throat.

"Who is in charge?" Alec's blazing topaz eyes challenged her with a look so darkly erotic, she shivered.

"You are," she purred, arching her pelvis upward.

"Aye." Alec pushed aside the hem of his kilt and entered Kate slowly until she adjusted to his size. Her hands closed over his muscular buttocks and her legs locked around his waist as she arched upward, taking in each driving stroke with giddy eagerness. The starched cotton of his shirt chafed her sore nipples and his wool kilt abraded her thighs as he surged inside her.

Kate teetered on the brink of madness as Alec made love to her like a man possessed, with such raw, primal passion, she could scarcely breathe. So delirious was she for all of him, she would have *begged* him not to stop if he had. His face strained, Alec held her face between his hands, his eyes boring into hers, obliging her to meet them. Her pelvis bucked beneath him, wanting more, *more*. And suddenly her soaring crescendo peaked and she imploded, careening wildly out of control.

She clutched Alec's tight buttocks until he reached a fierce climax and his deep voice rumbled out of his chest. "Kate, beautiful Kate, you've come back to me."

With a hoarse shudder, he withdrew and collapsed on his back, pulling her on top of him. She could hear his hammering heart as she pressed her cheek against his heaving chest. Kate kissed the hollow of his throat and slid a hand inside his open shirt, resting it over his heart.

Kate had no idea what time it was when she awakened. The commotion outside only meant one thing—Hogmanay was in full swing.

"Wake up," she said, patting Alec's face when he didn't open his eyes.

"What?" he said drowsily.

"It's Hogmanay."

"Happy New Year, beautiful," he said, kissing her temple.

"Happy New Year, handsome." Her fingers climbed his chest. "Aren't you going to do your duty?"

"What do you mean?"

"Maisie and Don told me about the first footing tradition where a tall, dark and handsome stranger arrives with a gift of coal to bring good luck to the New Year."

"And?" He pulled back and looked at her.

"It's time to do your duty, dark-haired Highlander. I'm suddenly famished and not for coal. Is there anything to eat here?"

Alec quirked a thick eyebrow. "Back to issuing orders, eh? I gave you something far better than coal."

"Aye, you did," she said, imitating his Scottish accent. She looked down and began to chuckle.

"What's so funny?"

"Look at us. My couture gown is bunched up around my waist and you're lying here with your kilt askew." She sat up and somehow managed to smooth her form-fitting skirt down past her knees. "There, that's better."

"It's a crime to cover you." Alec murmured huskily. "Let's get you out of the dress."

He turned Kate over and unzipped her evening gown, kissing her back and spine where the descending zipper revealed. He slid her dress off and Kate tried to turn over on her back, but he stopped her with a large hand splayed over her bottom.

"Not so fast, wee Katie." He chuckled wickedly. "Though I wouldn't exactly call you wee," he said with a lusty slap on her bottom.

Kate flailed her arm back to hit him. "You beast. Let me up," she huffed in mock outrage. She knew he was teasing; he'd always said he loved her curves.

"Hey, it's a compliment. You know I have a weakness for more than a handful, and you are gorgeous," he said, kissing the object of his affection.

"That's more like it," she said, pushing herself up on the elbows.

"Don't even think of moving a muscle. I'm not finished feasting on you."

And feast he did—to his heart's content—on the sensitive back of her nape, the indentations of her waist, the back of her knees, the curves of her buttocks, thighs and calves... He didn't stop until he'd lavished all of her with attention and she was blushing fiercely, biting the pillow.

"Sweetheart, you're more delectable than I remembered, if that's even possible," he said, giving her buttock a final nip before rising from the bed.

Kate turned on her back and fluffed a pillow under her head as she watched him strip off the white shirt revealing the corded muscles in his back. She loved the strong supple curve of his neck where it met his broad shoulders. Her pulse tripped up remembering how powerful his body had felt while he'd made love to her.

Alec walked to the bathroom and returned moments later, wearing a white hotel robe and carrying another for her. "Here, put this on. You don't want to miss the fireworks. Unless you'd rather stay in bed..." He grinned. "There were plenty of those here."

"I love your fireworks," Kate said, returning his grin.

She tucked into the plush bathrobe Alec handed her and joined him at the large window. He stood behind her, his arms wrapped snugly around her as they watched streaks of bright, electrical lights bursting into thistles and saltires that commemorated St. Andrew's cross. At a distance, Edinburgh castle glowed amidst the stunning pyrotechnic display. The midnight sky lit up everywhere as throngs of people sang *Auld Lang Syne* accompanied by the Scottish rock groups playing at a distance.

"What an awesome sight," Kate said.

"Aye, it's fantastic."

"How many people do you think are out there?"

"Last I heard they were expecting about 80,000. Too bad we missed the torch light procession through the city."

Kate leaned her head back against Alec's strong chest. "I'm not sorry we missed it. Coming together was far better," she said with a dreamy sigh.

"Agreed." Alec's warm hands slid inside Kate's robe and intimately caressed her breasts, his fingertips gently tugging the nipples. "You and I have some wee unfinished business, Katie."

"What do you mean?"

He kissed the side of her neck and nipped her earlobe, causing gooseflesh to rise on her neck and arms. With his dark head bent toward her, he murmured, "We need to come to an agreement."

Kate turned to face him. "About what?" she asked, her heart in her throat. *What he was feeling and thinking?* The force of his penetrating gaze unnerved her.

"Us…this." He slid his hands under her robe and clasped her buttocks, lifting her to his waist level. Kate wrapped her thighs around him and locked her feet behind his buttocks as he braced his legs and slid inside her.

She threw her head back and moaned with pleasure.

"I'm not letting you go again," he said, kissing the pulsing beat on her throat.

"Good," she said, loving the feel of his lips on her skin.

"We could be making a bairn tonight." His intense, glowing eyes held her prisoner as he began a slow and thorough plunder. "If we do, we'll raise him...or her *together*."

"Okay," she said, dazed and elated that he was onboard with having a baby with her.

"No more talk about fertility clinics," he said between measured, deliberate thrusts. His eyes held hers as he moved into her strongly. "The bairn will be mine. *Ours*."

"Ours," she agreed, gasping with pleasure.

He rocked his body against her, holding her captive and inexorably bound to him. Against the backdrop of the fireworks, Alec made love to her fiercely, passionately, until he wrung out a response so swift and startling she clung to him as if her life depended on it. His cry of release followed immediately afterward. Still embedded in her, he walked toward the bed supporting her weight with his palms as if she weighed nothing.

"Quick, make a wish," he whispered against her ear, hugging her tightly.

"A second chance for us?" Kate's heart constricted with longing as she dearly hoped he'd agree.

Alec kissed her tenderly, his lips like velvet against her mouth. "Aye, a second chance."

"I'll cherish this night forever," she whispered.

"There will be more nights like these...and days," Alec said huskily.

With all her heart, Kate wished she could believe him. She was terrified that emotionally she was where she'd vowed never to be again—vulnerable and worried about being abandoned. "Promise?" she asked softly, hating how needy she sounded.

He nodded.

"I don't want to be apart again," Kate said, her voice breaking as tears slid down her cheeks. "I hate that I have to leave tomorrow."

When they reached the bed, he gently disengaged and sat her on the bed. "Why do you have to leave so soon?"

Kate turned down the sheets and welcomed him in beside her. "My partner Evie is taking vacation, and before she leaves we have to complete a high-profile bridal order. I can't divulge who the client is. Let's just say she's an A list movie star."

Alec chuckled. "An A lister movie star, eh? Good for you."

"It's good for business," Kate said. "But I just wish I could stay longer…with you."

"Me too. But don't worry. I'll come to you," he said, smoothing her hair back.

Her heart soared with hope. "When can you come?" she said quickly.

"I'm not sure. I'll try to make it soon, but I can't say when just yet." He kissed the dampness from her cheeks. "No more tears now. We can't have you starting the New Year crying."

"They're happy tears," she said dreamily.

Later that night they made love again, savoring the mutual pleasuring at a slower pace. Afterward, Kate lay beside Alec with her face nestled in the crook of his neck, relishing the afterglow. His arm was draped over her waist as his hand leisurely stroked her hip.

Kate traced a heart on Alec's chest. "I'm so relieved," she said softly.

"Why?"

"I never thought I'd feel this way again. I was beginning to think something was wrong with me. After you left, I never felt like this toward anyone. I have only loved you," she said sincerely.

Alec hugged her tightly. "Ah, Katie, beautiful Katie. I've loved you since the day I saw you in that English pub, dressing down the bartender for being rude to a handicapped client. I love the grit you're made of." His warm hand gently massaged her back, strong and proprietary. "Underneath your soft skin is an iron will. I admire the woman you've become, the way you selflessly raised your brothers into fine men."

"Thank you, but sometimes I wish I didn't have to be strong all the time." She closed her eyes, remembering the happiest moment in her life. When she and Alec eloped. "The first time I ever felt free was when we got married. By then the boys were grown and fending for themselves...and they loved you. You were a good role model. Someone to look up to."

"I always felt bad about how they were affected by our divorce. I wanted to keep in touch, but you refused to let me."

Kate tilted her head to look up at him. "A clean break was better. I was too scared that you'd disappear from their lives too. I was protecting them."

"A mother lioness. Someday you're going to make an amazing mother," he said, kissing her forehead.

"I hope so. I really do," she said, touched to the core of her soul. She gazed at his strong profile, loving the way he looked after their lovemaking—relaxed and content. She placed a gentle hand on his cheek. "Alec?"

"Aye?" He peered at her from beneath thick, sable lashes.

"I don't want to keep anything from you. We should be honest with each other, right?"

He turned on his side to face her. "What's this about, Katie?"

"There's something important I need to tell you." She struggled to find the right words as the sad memory filled her heart. "Years ago, I had a miscarriage. It was your baby."

"When?"

"I found out I was pregnant after our divorce and a month later I miscarried."

His eyes glowed in the dim light coming in from the window. "Why didn't you tell me?"

"You had already disappeared."

One dark brow rose. "You could have reached me through Eileen. I would have come back to you."

"That's exactly why I didn't. I wanted you to come back because you loved me, not because of a sense of duty. Or because you felt sorry for me."

He gave the barest sigh, but it spoke volumes. "You still should have told me, Katie," he said, his voice laced with reproach.

"Don't you understand how much I was hurting? It was bad enough I lost you, but I lost our baby too!"

Alec nodded and after a pause, let out a heavy sigh. "I'm sorry you had to cope with the miscarriage alone. And all because of my stupid, stubborn pride. I should have come back to you after we divorced and tried to make it work." He tilted her face up and kissed her tenderly. "I love you."

He still loved her. *Thank God.* Kate gazed at him, her heart filled with wonder. "You won't ever lose me," she vowed. "I'm yours. Forever."

They talked for hours into the early morning about a lot of things, sharing past disappointments and commiserating over lost time together. It hadn't been all serious. They'd laughed too. Alec enjoyed teasing her and making her giggle. And she loved teasing him back.

They never discussed the details on how they'd begin their second chance at love. But sometime during that long, passionate night, the fight that had ignited their fierce coupling transformed into tender passion and mutual respect as they came full circle.

CHAPTER SIX

Kate woke up feeling disoriented. Her mouth was parched and her stomach a bit woozy, even though she was hungry for breakfast. For a moment, she didn't know where she was as she tried to focus in the dark room. She turned on her side and stared at the large windows. The massive drapes were drawn, blackening the room. A glance at her smartphone on the nightstand told her it was 9:00 am. She had spent most of the night in Alec's arms, she recalled with a satiated smile.

She was lying on the softest sheets she'd ever slept on, in a big, comfy bed and her mind was inundated with the most delicious, sensual memories—ones that would last a lifetime. But at the moment, she was alone and the most important person in her life was missing—Alec.

Kate groped the area beside her on the bed even though she knew Alec wasn't there. She would have felt his large presence if he had. Something was off. She sat up and winced at the ache in her temples. She shouldn't have knocked back those two whiskeys last night. *Bad move.* Now she was in for a bitch of a headache. Her stomach didn't feel that great either. A hot cup of strong Earl Grey tea was exactly what she needed to revive herself.

She pulled on the robe and padded to the bathroom on bare feet, hoping Alec might be there. Kate knocked on the door and called out Alec's name a few times. When he didn't answer, she opened the door and was surprised to find he'd already showered and had used his shaving kit.

She went back into the room and switched on the lights. After a quick search, she saw Alec's formalwear hanging in the closet. His suitcase was there too.

Where was he?

Alec briskly strolled through the streets of Edinburgh, welcoming the cold morning air that assailed his face. For the most part, the streets were cleaned up after the revelry of Hogmanay. It was a gray morning with no sun in sight, but Alec didn't mind. He was used to inclement winter weather. He would have walked in rain or snow. There was no better place than outdoors to pull his thoughts together. He needed time alone to mentally digest everything and clear the sensual fog of his night with Katie. He had never felt so connected to anyone.

The moment he made love to her, Alec knew he loved Katie as much he had before—perhaps more. He felt humbled by her honesty, the way she'd bared her soul to him. *I never thought I'd feel this way again. I was beginning to think something was wrong with me. After you left, I never felt like this toward anyone. I have only loved you.*

During their heartfelt conversations, he understood better her need to be in control. It was self-preservation more than anything. Katie was feisty and strong-willed, qualities he wouldn't change for the world. She'd always owned his heart and thinking about her now made him want her even more.

The moment he'd seen her at the church the reality hit him full force. He'd missed Katie much more than he was willing to admit. She had his heart, had always had his heart, even from the moment he met her in a pub. She'd been so busy reproaching the rude bartender, she hadn't noticed Alec until he handed her a mug of ale. He'd been a damned idiot to leave her. They could have worked something out, but he'd been too hot-headed.

The confounding reality was that it might not be only about him and Kate. There was a possibility of a bairn. His bairn. The thought terrified him and thrilled him at once. It would bring an immediate change to his lifestyle. At thirty-eight, he had everything in the world he could ask for but one thing—love. All that would change now. Reuniting with Katie was the first step.

If they'd made a bairn last night, great. If not, he'd always have Katie. All night they'd had steamy, unprotected sex that had been amazing. But what had drawn him to her was the intimate conversation that followed. The emotional closeness with Katie had been a balm, healing the past sorrows of the year and giving him newfound hope. Maybe, just maybe they could make things work this time. If last night was any indication, he was willing to try.

He'd been surprised when she had told him she was ovulating, but that according to her doctor she might have trouble conceiving. *That's why I wanted you to donate sperm. For more chances*, she'd said.

Alec had told her in no uncertain terms that if she wanted more chances, he would provide them—in person. She'd laughed at that and agreed wholeheartedly. Thank God she'd come to him and not a fertility clinic. The minute she'd flung it in his face, he knew he was a goner. There was no way he'd allow her to carry any man's bairn but his. Having kids wasn't part of his plan. He was stunned at the confidence he'd felt when he made the decision to give Katie what she wanted. He'd known then as he did now, it was the right thing—for them.

Alec had been living autonomously for a long time and he'd enjoyed the liberty to come and go without strings. Just before the wedding he'd decided to go back into active duty doing investigations and covert operations. He'd been out of the field for a while, but after he'd caught the mob members threatening the Broadway star, Natasha White, he'd gotten a strong rush of adrenaline—the kind that made him forget everything, and he'd needed it badly. Still reeling from his parents' death and his beloved granny's passing all in one year, he had wanted to escape his melancholy by jumping back in the saddle.

For the past five years, he had been working at the helm of his personal security company and not in the trenches, building his company into a highly lucrative business. He hadn't told Kate that he'd be gone on the next mission starting today. Last night had been just for them. To reconnect and catch up; to make up for all lost time by making love all night. He hadn't brought it up because he knew she would instantly recoil at the possibility of him being in danger.

I don't want to keep anything from you. We should be honest with each other, right? The reality of Kate's words slapped him in the face. Bloody hell, he would have never signed up if he'd known they were getting back together. Now that he'd have someone to come home to and that there was a possibility of a bairn, he needed to rethink the missions.

But first he needed to come clean with Katie. He owed her that much. He smiled to himself as a plan developed. First he'd stop at Jasper's and pick up Katie's favorite scones, almond blackberry. He would order a special breakfast and by the time he got back to the hotel, it would be there waiting for them. Then he'd break the news...gently.

He could just imagine her in bed waiting for him, all creamy curves and fragrant skin, with her tousled golden brown hair spread on the pillows. He got a tantalizing vision of round, pale breasts with petal pink tips, of curved hips and supple thighs. He grew instantly hard. She'd been so delicious last night, so uninhibited. To hell with breakfast. He'd rather devour Katie, he thought grinning with anticipation.

Alec glanced at his watch. 9:30 a.m. By now she would be awake. Damn, he hadn't thought of getting her cell number to let her know he'd be back soon. He should have left a note. He dialed the hotel and asked to be connected to his suite.

The phone rang at least twenty times before it went back to the front desk clerk.

"Please try again," Alec told him.

"Do you want to be connected to voice mail if there's no answer?" the clerk asked.

"No thanks."

Alec impatiently listened as the phone rang a long time. Where the bloody hell was Katie? He hoped she wasn't in the shower. Well…if she was, he'd just have to kiss the droplets of water off her fragrant body.

He punched redial. "Please connect me with my suite again," Alec told the clerk.

The phone rang and rang, but still no answer. Why wasn't Katie answering?

Kate never thought she'd be doing the walk of shame in a wrinkled, jade satin gown. But there she was stuck in an elevator with a family of four—a tall, skinny man hiding a smile, his short, stout wife bristling with indignation and two teenage girls gawking at her. Kate stood rigid with embarrassment as she stared fixedly at the elevator buttons.

The moment the elevator doors opened on her floor, she bolted out and ran down the hall to her room. She took a quick shower and then got ready for her trip. It didn't take long to pack her gown in the suitcase. Since she knew she'd be flying out today, she had tidied up her room and pre-packed everything before going to the wedding. She changed into a soft black cashmere sweater and black skinny jeans and slipped on the dangling silver and amethyst teardrop earrings Alec had surprised her with many years ago.

She scribbled a note with all her contact information. She put on red lipstick and kissed the bottom of the card before slipping it back in the envelope. She left it with the front desk clerk for Alec. Once Alec read it, he'd get the message.

During the taxi ride to the airport, Kate opened the window and gulped in mouthfuls of cold, damp air. The shock of frigid air bolstered her and she didn't feel so anxious...just sad and letdown. She had hoped to say good-by to Alec, and the fact that he'd left her alone to go God knows where made her more than a little nervous.

Alec had agreed to give them a second chance last night. Had he only done it to have sex with her? *No!* She refused to believe he had lied to her, not after the beautiful night they'd spent. He would never be that cruel. Alec might be hot-headed and stubborn, but he was noble. Maybe he had panicked at the commitment they'd made and decided to cut out before she got more attached to the idea of having a baby. As much as it made her heart squeeze and her stomach tighten, she had to trust him. She didn't want to go back to her usual pattern of self-denial for self-preservation.

After she went through security a thought occurred to her. Maybe there was still hope...maybe, just maybe he'd show up at the airport like one of those romantic comedy heroes who raced against the clock to stop his girlfriend from leaving at the airport. And then in front of everyone, he'd loudly proclaim his love by proposing to her on his knees.

Fat chance. She was being naïve and silly hoping for that scenario. But she couldn't help wishing that she'd look up and find Alec coming toward her with love all over his rugged face. *Katie, you're not leaving here. You're mine. You will always be mine.* What she'd give to hear him say that! She scanned the terminal again, hoping she'd spot him. She squinted, looking right and left, over her shoulder, but came up empty. She was trying to hold onto the hope that he'd make it in time so they could say good-bye in person.

Yesterday, he'd told her he wasn't planning on getting married and she'd replied she wasn't asking him to. *What a hypocrite.* The moment she saw him standing at the entrance of the church, Kate regretted their divorce more than anything in the world. Then when he made love to her so passionately, so fiercely, she vowed never to be separated from him again. She relived the tenderness of his kisses, the way he'd looked at her as if she were the most beautiful woman in the world.

Her heart melted remembering his words. *Ah, Katie, beautiful Katie. I've loved you since the day I saw you in that English pub, dressing down the bartender for being rude to a handicapped client. I should have come back to you after we divorced, but my stubborn pride held me back. I don't ever want to lose you.*

She knew Alec would come. He had to. After the kind of night they'd spent and the beautiful things he'd said to her, there was no way he'd let her leave without saying good-bye. It was a two hour wait before the flight, ample time for Alec to make it.

Two hours later, Kate stood at the gate alone with a lump in her throat. She had finally stopped looking over her shoulder. Her heart sank even lower as she removed her earrings and put them in her handbag. Alec wasn't going to show up. The reality hit her full-force.

Don't cry. Not one tear or you won't be able to stop the meltdown. She fought back her tears and forced herself into the plane.

CHAPTER SEVEN

Kate downed the last of her lemongrass green tea and rinsed her cup before joining Evie at the front parlor of their bridal boutique. "Where's the shipment of ring pillows we ordered?"

"It's right there, next to the display case. I haven't gotten a chance to put them away yet," Evie said, looking up from her computer.

"I'll do it."

Evie took off her hipster glasses and studied her. "Are you finally going to tell me what happened?"

"No."

"Come on, Kate. I'm worried about you." Evie's dark blue eyes looked exasperated as she ran a hand through her jet black pixie length hair.

"Don't be." Kate trudged to the cardboard box on the floor. "I'll survive."

"Maybe. But it's been two weeks since you came back and you haven't told me anything about your trip, other than the bride looked beautiful." She paused. "I know something is eating at you. You look absolutely miserable."

"I don't want to talk about it," Kate said tightly as she took the tiny pillows out of the box. If she opened up, she'd start bawling. She hadn't heard from Alec. Not one peep. She still couldn't wrap her head around it. How could he disappear like that? *Without a trace.* Part of her was petrified that something terrible had happened to him. The other part wanted to murder him for breaking her heart again.

"You can't keep everything bottled up like that. It's not good for you."

"Quit nagging, Evie! I said I don't want to talk about it." Kate stacked the pillows side by side and punched each one in the middle.

"Hey, don't bite my head off and please don't gut the pillows. Is Mercury in retrograde? Are you PMSing or something? This isn't like you."

Kate whirled around. "You really want to know what's wrong?"

Evie nodded vigorously. "Yes. Please!"

Kate stalked to the antique ivory and gold desk and plopped down in the armchair in front of it. She took a deep breath and exhaled sharply. "Fine. I'll tell you. I went to Scotland, reunited with my ex-husband, made love all night and then he disappeared. End of story." Hot tears formed at the back of her eyes. She blinked rapidly not to let them escape.

"Oh, honey. I'm so sorry." Evie's multi-ringed hand rested over Kate's and gave it a gentle squeeze.

"Don't be. I should have known better. I'm an idiot," Kate said, dashing a tear. Her throat was thick with grief.

"No you're not. You're the smartest person I know," Evie said indignantly. "What happened?"

Might as well come clean. The burden of her pain might eased by sharing it with Evie. She loved Evie like a sister. Maybe she could help her figure out what to do next. Kate shook her head mournfully. "This is going to sound weird."

"Not from you, it won't," Evie said supportively.

"Okay, here goes. I know you won't judge," she said with a sigh. "I promised myself I'd stay strong when I saw Alec. I only wanted one thing from him. A baby."

Evie's eyes shot open and her mouth dropped. "A baby? I had no idea. *Wow*," she breathed. "With all the men you could have chosen, why on earth would you pick your ex? I thought your marriage ended badly...so badly that you hadn't seen or talked to him since. And you always said it was mutual...that he didn't want anything to do with you. It was very brave of you to reach out to him, Kate." She stared at her in awe. "He could have turned you down flat."

"Not brave. A fool for love. I desperately wanted to have a baby. Alec's baby." She paused. "And he did turn me down...at first."

Wide-eyed, Evie nodded and remained silent.

Kate lifted one shoulder in a self-conscious shrug. "I only asked for his sperm donation. When he balked, I said I'd go to a sperm bank. Being the way he is, he'd have none of that and seduced me. I lost my head again. I have no control when it comes to him."

Evie regarded her with sympathy as she smiled gently. "Don't beat yourself up, Kate. I know exactly how you feel. That's how it was with Michael...until he passed. I don't know if I'll ever find someone as amazing as my late husband."

Kate shot up from the chair and hugged her. "Oh, Evie. I'm so sorry. I know how much you miss Michael." Evie was so beautiful with her shiny dark hair and pink-cheeked, porcelain complexion. She was even more beautiful inside and it pained Kate that she worried she'd never find someone to love again.

Evie's wide blue eyes welled up with tears. She brushed them away with a sheepish smile. "It's been seven years, but I think of Michael every day... and night. I don't think I'll ever get over losing him."

Evie's grief was so palpable, Kate stopped feeling sorry for herself and straightened up. "I'll help you find happiness again," she said, hoping with all her heart she was right. "We will both start over. We can't end up like the Golden Girls." She forced a smile to cheer her up.

Evie gave a half-hearted chuckle. "Don't even think that. I just had a vision of us, old and gray, in our flannel nightgowns watching T.V." She got up and grabbed her oversized python leather tote. "Let's get out of here. No more feeling sorry for ourselves. Come to my place. I'll cook dinner for us."

"Pasta?" Kate asked eagerly. Evie was part Italian on her dad's side and her pasta dishes were delicious.

"Yep. I'll cook us up so much comfort food you won't be able to move," Evie said, snickering.

"I don't doubt it. I love your cooking," Kate said. "Go on without me. There's something I must do first. I'll join you soon."

"Ok, but don't take too long. I'm starving," Evie said before she walked out the door.

Once Evie had gone, Kate opened her tote bag and pulled out a plastic bag. Her heart was beating so fast it felt like palpitations. She had been postponing this all day...too scared to find out. But now that she had gathered the courage, she couldn't wait another minute. She had to know...one way or the other. On shaky legs and with her heart in her throat, she walked toward the bathroom.

Moments later, Kate stood in front of the bathroom mirror, staring at her pale, incredulous face. Lightheaded, she clutched the pregnancy test with a trembling hand and swallowed hard to stifle the giddy gasp rising from her chest.

She kissed her hand and placed it over her tummy. "Welcome baby MacLeod," she whispered. "I love you already."

CHAPTER EIGHT

Kate entered her bridal boutique with a bounce to her step and a purpose in her life. She'd spent the past two days fluctuating between panicking over whether she was fit to be a single mother, agonizing over Alec's whereabouts and sheer joy that she was going to have a baby. After much reflection and hours of talking with Evie, she decided all that worrying was bad for the baby.

It was time to *suck it up, buttercup*. Life wasn't about her anymore. By next time this year, she would be holding her baby in her arms. The thought sent shivers of delight and anxiety racing through her. What would her pregnancy be like? Would she be able to carry full-term? She was determined to eat healthy, sleep as much as possible and stay away from stress.

"Hey hot momma," Evie teased the moment she saw Kate. "How was last night?"

Kate smiled. "Better. Much better. Thanks for the ear."

"Anytime. Just remember I am your baby's favorite auntie. I'll be your birthing coach too, if you want me to. Breathe in, breathe out, relax," she said dramatically, her eyes twinkling merrily.

"You would be my birthing coach? Thank you!" Kate hugged Evie, silently vowing to bring her happiness too. Her new mission would be to find someone for Evie. "Would you be the godmother too?"

Evie's face lit up brighter than the chandelier above. "Absolutely. I'm honored you chose me."

"I can't think of anyone else I'd want to raise my baby if I were gone," Kate said honestly.

"Thanks, but please don't think like that."

"I have to think of those things as a single mom," Kate said earnestly.

"I hear you. Always the practical one," she said with a smile. "We have a new client coming in soon. Good thing you came in early."

An hour later, Evie entered the small kitchen while Kate was having a mid-morning strawberry, banana and yogurt smoothie. "Kate, the client is here."

"Oh, okay." Kate took a final sip of her smoothie and smoothed the sides of her dress as she walked toward the front of the salon.

The moment she saw him, Kate's heart stood still and blood drained from her face. The last person in the world she expected to see at the entrance of her bridal boutique was Alec. Yet there he was in flesh and blood, staring at her with a remorseful expression. A wave of dizziness made Kate clutch the display case beside her.

"Katie. Sweetheart," Alec said, walking toward her with outstretched arms.

"Stay away," Kate blurted out, grabbing the closest thing to her. A crystal and pearl tiara. She brandished it in the air. "I'm not afraid to use this and I will, MacLeod. To bash your thoughtless, despicable, inconsiderate, selfish…" She furiously searched for more words as he stealthily approached her. But she came up empty. She was so shocked—and profoundly relieved to see him—she couldn't get past the last word.

Evie jumped up from her chair and managed to topple the stack of bridal albums on the antique desk. They landed in a heap at Alec's feet. "Wait a minute. You're Alec MacLeod? *The* Alec MacLeod?" Evie ran her fingers through her short hair until it stood out in spikes, creating a Statue of Liberty type crown.

"Aye." Not taking his eyes off Kate, Alec continued to head toward her.

Evie grabbed her tote bag and headed out the door. "I'll give you two some privacy. Call me later, Kate."

By the time Alec reached Kate's side, she was beside herself. She took several steadying breaths and forced air into her constricting lungs.

"What are you doing here?" she finally said, filled with despair over her heart's treacherous reaction. She was so thankful he was alive, she could barely hold onto her anger over his disappearance.

"I came to apologize."

"Two weeks later?" she asked incredulously. Feelings of betrayal and distrust reared up inside her as she trembled. "Are you freaking kidding me? You expect me to welcome you with open arms? I don't want to hear anything you have to say."

He made a helpless gesture with his hand. "I'm sorry, Katie."

"Ha!" she said, infusing it with as much scorn as she could muster.

"Really, I am sorry. I was on a covert mission."

The cords in Kate's neck felt swollen as she tried to get a grip. "And you couldn't call me or even send a message to let me know you were alive?"

"Not bloody likely. On a mission, there's no contact with anyone until it's over." His face strained, he pinched the bridge of his nose. "When you hear what I have to say, you'll change your mind."

"I doubt it. I thought you were either dead or ditched me after the night we spent."

A muscle in his jaw clenched. "I never ditched you."

"Yes, you did! I couldn't even call Eileen to find out if you were okay. She was on her honeymoon with her *considerate* husband while I was agonizing over your safety. *Damn you,*" she said, fighting tears.

"I love you."

"No, you don't. Go away," she said when he took a step toward her.

"I love you," he repeated. His hands closed over her waist and he lifted her up until they were eye level. His eyes flicked over her before boring into hers. She recognized that look in his eyes and shivered inside. The wicked gleam said he was this close to throwing her over his shoulder and carting her to the back room for some hot, make up sex.

"Don't you dare go caveman on me, MacLeod. It's not good for the baby," Katie snapped. "Put me down."

Alec's dark brows shot up as his eyes popped open. He set her down gently. "What did you just say?"

"I said it's not good for the baby. I'm pregnant," she said, relishing the look of astonishment on his face.

Alec's face instantly split into a wide grin. She had never seen him look so elated and it made her heart ache. He carefully folded her in his arms as if she were carrying precious cargo…and she was. "I'm so happy, sweetheart," he whispered hoarsely.

Kate put a hand on his chest and extricated herself. She shook her head and swiped at hot tears. "No, Alec, I can't allow my child to have even one moment of panic that her daddy won't be there for her, that one day he'll leave and never come back. I know how awful that feels."

"That would never happen," he said grittily. "It was the last mission I'll ever be on. I resigned from active service."

"You did?" She searched his face, hoping with all her heart he meant it. Her profound, aching resentment began to subside, but she couldn't have Alec coming into and out of her life like that. "You're not planning on taking another dangerous assignment?"

"No." Alec's eyes bored into hers with such intensity she blinked. "I was planning to tell you about the last assignment the morning after the wedding," he said, drawing in a rough breath. "I had bought your favorite scones and was on my way back to the hotel when I got sidetracked."

She put her hands on her hips and squinted up at him. "By what? What could have been more important?"

His eyes were troubled as he looked at her. "An old lady was hit by a drunk on a bike who claimed he didn't see her until it was too late. The scunner must have been drinking all night. She was in bad shape and I stayed with her until the ambulance arrived. I kept calling the hotel to tell you, but there was no answer in my room or yours."

"I wish you had come to the airport." Her lower lip quivered. "I waited for hours hoping you would."

Alec's eyes clouded with a stricken look. "Believe me I would have, but it was too late by the time I got back."

"Did the hotel clerk give you my note?" she asked, reliving how vulnerable she'd felt when she left it. She felt even more vulnerable now.

"Aye. That's why I'm here. It was the most beautiful message I've ever read. *I have loved you forever. Wherever you are, I'll be there*," he said repeating what she'd written. He knelt before her and kissed the top of her stomach. "And now we're having a bairn, I'll never leave your side, sweetheart."

Her mouth went dry. "Promise?"

"I promise," he said, rising to his feet. He pulled Kate into his arms and kissed her.

Her heart expanded in her chest with joy. Kate's eyes welled up with tears as she rested her head on his chest and nestled in his solid embrace. She was where she belonged, in Alec's arms and next to his heart. She could hear his heart pounding strongly, reminding her of the new life she carried. Their New Year baby.

"If it's a boy, we'll call him Robbie," she said, her voice breaking.

"Thank you," he whispered hoarsely.

"And if it's a girl, we'll name her Elizabeth after your granny," she said, happy tears wetting the front of his shirt.

"That would be great. It means the world to me, Katie," he said, hugging her tightly.

"And to me," she said smiling up at him.

"There's just one thing missing, sweetheart. I want to take care of you, to give you and our bairn all my love.

Forever." His glowing leonine eyes held hers captive as he pulled out a little Tiffany box and opened it to reveal a large, square cut diamond surrounded by emeralds. "Will you marry me? Will you be mine, Katie?"

She stared at him in wonder. Her heart expanded in her chest with so much happiness it was almost unbearable. Unblinking, Kate met his steady gaze and saw herself in his eyes. Saw how much he loved her. Saw his soul bared in the depths of those beautiful eyes.

"I've always been yours, Alec. You know that. Of course I'll marry you!" she said, throwing her arms around him. "By this time next year there will be three of us."

"This is just the beginning, sweetheart. We'll have a houseful of bairns if you want."

"Yes, at least two more," she said, drinking in his exuberant kisses.

Once she caught her breath from his ardent kisses, her forehead creased. "Alec?"

"What is it?" he said, searching her face.

"Can we find a husband for Evie too? All this happiness makes me want others to be happy too."

He drew back, his brow furrowed as he gave her a curious look. "Who's Evie?"

"My best friend." She chuckled. "The one we chased out of here."

"Ah, that one. Sure, sweetheart, anything to make you happy," he said hugging her tightly.

Thank you!

Thanks for reading *Heart Tamer,* I hope you enjoyed it!

- Reviews help other readers discover books, and I appreciate all reviews.
- For new release information and party information, sign up for my newsletter here: http://www.sophiaknightly.net/newsletter-sign-up.html
- If you'd like to read an excerpt of *Heart Melter,* the full length novel that precedes *Heart Tamer,* please turn the page.

Excerpt: Heart Melter

by Sophia Knightly

Chapter One

"You're flat," Simon called out from the third row of the dark theatre.

"No, I'm not." Natasha White gritted her teeth and raised a challenging eyebrow at the director. Her hands curved on the waist of her fawn satin teddy as she tamped down her simmering temper. Simon Worth was referring to her pitch, not her breasts, although he had spent most of the morning ogling them while she danced. It was the third time he'd rudely interrupted her song, and he'd made Freddie the choreographer change her tap number so many times, her muscles were screaming in protest. But she ignored the pain; it was worth having the starring role of Legs LaRue in "The Bee's Knees", a new roaring twenties musical sure to be a Broadway hit.

Simon was pushing hard during dress rehearsal—unfairly so. But what else could she expect from the control freak who had written the songs and lyrics of "The Bee's Knees" and was also directing it? The thirty-nine-year-old musical genius was temperamental and rude, but that wouldn't have stopped Natasha's mother, legendary Broadway diva, Anitra White, from letting loose a rant that would have singed Simon's bushy black brows. Where her acerbic mother would have screamed, Natasha held her tongue, even if she felt like strangling Simon. She didn't want any comparisons with her drama queen mama, not now, not ever.

"She was pitch perfect," her accompanist, Bruce, said instantly. Her white-haired defender pushed his horn rimmed glasses up on his high-bridged nose and glared at Simon. Bruce was an experienced, old school Broadway accompanist and nobody dared contradict him, not even Simon.

"Sounded gorgeous to me. Piss off, Simon." Freddie the choreographer's jaw clenched beneath his trim salt-and-pepper goatee as he sent a supportive nod Natasha's way. He had already had a meltdown this morning over Simon's intrusive meddling in his choreography. His compact dancer's body was coiled tightly, ready to spring on the director if he continued to bully Natasha. Not that she needed protecting. If she could handle her mother's tough criticism all those years growing up, she could certainly endure Simon's.

"Thanks, guys," Natasha said, blowing them kisses. She alternately rolled her neck and shoulders, and then peered into the theatre, her gaze zeroing in on her understudy, Lisette Raye, who watched with rabid ambition.

It was no secret Lisette was hot for the starring role— and the director. The pushy twenty-one-year-old actress and Simon were already sleeping together. Once he'd plowed through the ensemble and slept with most of them, Simon settled on Lisette, who eagerly pleased him in *all* areas. Well, she could have the pompous gasbag. Musical genius or not, he didn't appeal to Natasha, and she'd be damned if she'd sleep her way to the top. She'd seen too many failed "showmances"—mostly hook-ups that thrived during shows, but rarely made it past the last curtain call. Hanging around backstage as a child during her mom's Broadway shows had taught her to steer clear of romances in the business. It had also toughened her enough to let Simon's insults slide and not affect her performance.

"Let's take it from the top, and this time make sure your E makes me weep," Simon drawled caustically, ignoring the collective groans from Bruce and Freddie.

An hour later when Elisha, the stage manager, called lunch break, Natasha fled the theatre intent on grabbing a bite to eat and taking her Pomeranian puppy, Evita, for a quick walk. Evita was a gift from her childhood friend, Ronnie, and Ronnie's gorgeous new husband, Nick Cameron. They'd given her the puppy before leaving on their honeymoon. The moment the puppy emitted a melodious, crooning howl while Natasha sang, she promptly named her Evita, after the musical.

Natasha hurried across Times Square, her nerves frayed from Simon's heedless interruptions and unwarranted criticisms. Something wasn't right; she could feel it in her bones. Thinking back to her horoscope this morning, maybe she should heed Sydney Taggert's advice: *Keep an eye on your back and an eye toward the future.*

She zipped her tan leather jacket against the blast of ice cold air swirling around her. A bit early for such frigid weather in October, but everything this month seemed off. She usually made her way home at a brisk trot, but today her leg and butt muscles quivered from the morning's repetitive variations of the same dance. She was used to grueling workouts, but Simon had gone overboard. It was almost as if he were trying to push her to the breaking point. Well, it wasn't going to happen. He had underestimated the kind of grit she had developed over the years. She wasn't about to relinquish the plum role of Legs LaRue to a greedy newbie like Lisette.

With her head bent forward and her heavy dance tote slung across her chest, Natasha wove through the teeming crowd of tourists. She was two blocks away from her apartment when she felt a firm jerk on her dance bag. As she grappled to hold onto it and not lose her footing, a sharp pain sliced across her outer right thigh.

"Ouch!" She craned her neck to the side to see where the jab had come from. A quick glance at her leg made her gasp at the slash in her jeans and the long red line on her skin revealed by the gaping fabric. Within seconds blood rose to the cut's surface. With shaky hands, Natasha pulled her long knit scarf off her neck and tied it tightly around her upper thigh, forming a tourniquet to stop the bleeding.

She stepped onto the curb and frantically hailed a taxi. Within seconds, a cab drove up and she clambered inside.

"Where to?" the driver asked, turning to stare at her when she didn't answer right away.

Natasha could barely breathe, let alone speak as she stared at the driver. She swallowed and said through trembling lips, "Take me to the closest emergency clinic."

No, that wouldn't do. If she went to an emergency clinic, she'd be there all day. With Simon's foul mood and Lisette itching for her starring role, Natasha had to get back to rehearsal ASAP.

When the driver turned on 40th Street onto 6th Avenue, she remembered Ian's medical clinic was on that street. Her heart leaped at the thought of seeing her ex-fiancé again and it brought an onslaught of painful memories. Given the way they'd split up seven years ago, would he even agree to see her? At this crucial moment, who cared? She needed his expertise and who better than brilliant renowned cosmetic surgeon, Dr. Ian MacGregor, to treat her wound and not leave a disfiguring scar?

Knowing Ian, he'd take care of her too. He was a doctor first and foremost. Years ago, he'd been strong and protective of her…and they'd been passionately in love. Did she really want to go there after struggling for seven years to get him out of her heart? How would he react to her unexpected visit? She'd soon find out, she thought, quaking inside as she made a rash decision.

When she recognized Ian's building, she told the driver, "Stop here. Please. I'm getting off." She handed him a ten dollar bill and bolted out of the cab.

Inside the building, Natasha gulped air and tried not to look at her wound as she pressed the elevator button. Thankfully, it was empty and she rode up to Ian's office alone. But the moment she entered the reception area, she panicked at the roomful of patients waiting to be seen. Summoning strength—and courage—she limped toward the counter and tried not to put too much pressure on her injured leg.

"Excuse me," she said to a gray haired woman whose narrowed gaze was fixed on the computer screen before her. "I need to see Dr. MacGregor."

"Do you have an appointment?"

"No, but it's an emergency."

"I'm sorry. Dr. MacGregor doesn't take walk-ins," the woman replied briskly. Her name tag said Carla and Natasha wondered if she was the office manager.

"But I'm hurt," Natasha said, her voice rising in anguish. She motioned to her injured leg, hoping Carla would take pity on her.

"You're bleeding! You need to go to an emergency center. Now!" Carla said with a disapproving shake of her head.

A collective gasp sounded behind her and Natasha didn't need to turn around to confirm that all attention was riveted on her, from the buzzing voices of waiting patients to the concerned faces behind the glass reception counter.

She leaned forward and clutched the counter. "I don't feel very well. Please tell Dr. MacGregor that Natasha White needs to see him. He knows me."

"I can't interrupt him while he's with a patient," Carla said firmly.

Natasha closed her eyes and drew in calming breaths. How on earth was she going to get past Ian's gatekeeper to see him? *Desperate times called for desperate measures.* She swayed on her feet and collapsed, making sure to land carefully on her uninjured side. Good thing her acting classes had included pratfalls, she thought wryly, as she lay on the floor pretending to be unconscious.

Carla rounded the corner immediately. "Good Lord! She fainted. Get Dr. MacGregor. Quick!" she yelled, patting Natasha's cheek.

Seconds later, Natasha heard a deep male voice say, "What's going on, Carla?" He reached Natasha's side in seconds. "Tasha? Oh God. What happened?"

The hairs on Natasha's arms stood on end and butterflies swarmed her belly at the sound of Ian's rich voice, resonant with a Scottish burr. She opened her eyes and slowly met his—silver-green wolf eyes densely rimmed with sooty black lashes. Her heart pounded riotously as his arresting gaze locked with hers and a familiar weakness overcame her making it hard to breathe.

Ian's sheer male force engulfed her, held her in thrall as she lay before him, almost sick with anticipation of his next move. A jumble of potent emotions blindsided her. Longing, excitement, trepidation, despair. She hadn't realized how much seeing him again would affect her and she needed a moment to pull herself together.

Natasha closed her eyes and let her body go limp again.

Muttering "bloody hell", Ian lifted her up and carried her down the hallway and into a room. She didn't dare open her eyes. *Please let him think I'm unconscious,* she thought, mortified she'd had to resort to fainting like a damsel in distress. Before Ian, of all people.

He gently deposited her on the examining table and made short work of removing her jeans with the help of a nurse named Judy. While the nurse cleaned the wound,

Ian examined it and Natasha kept her eyes closed the whole time.

"It's superficial. I'll take it from here, Judy. Please go to Mrs. Phillips in room six. I'll be there shortly."

"Yes, Doc," Judy said and hustled out of the room.

"Nobody faints for that long. Open your eyes, Tasha," Ian said in a voice laden with irony.

Tasha. Hearing Ian's pet name for her made Natasha's heart squeeze. Her lashes fluttered as she blinked at the bright lights and focused on Ian's face. He loomed above her, handsome as ever with a straight, aristocratic nose, a firm jaw and sensual lips that rivaled any Michelangelo statue. Thick dark brows formed straight slashes above narrowed crystal green eyes that raked over her with concern. Ian's vibrant wolf eyes stirred her blood and a tremor coursed through her as his steady gaze held her immobile.

"Ian." Natasha took a deep breath of the sterile air in a fruitless attempt to calm her racing heart. "I...I..." she stammered.

Ian arched one brow and stared at her meaningfully.

She rubbed her arms against the shivery sensations he aroused, fervently hoping he couldn't tell how unhinged she felt. She stared back, trapped in his penetrating gaze. For the life of her, she couldn't think of anything to say. He had to be wondering if she'd lost her marbles.

"I'm sorry I passed out and bled all over your carpet out there. I'll have it replaced," she finally managed to say. She held her breath and waited for Ian to do something. A smile, a frown—anything to break the crackling tension between them.

Ian's mouth tightened. "I don't care about the bloody carpet. Let's turn you on your left side so I can tend to the cut." He placed a supporting hand on Natasha's upper back and carefully eased her onto her side.

The moment his warm skin touched hers, gooseflesh spread on Natasha's sensitized skin and zips of excitement shot to her pleasure points. It had always been like this with him. Ian's touch or a look from his heated eyes was all it took to set her aflame.

She huffed for air before meeting his gaze. "I probably shouldn't have come here, but I don't trust anyone else with my legs. You're the best." The moment the words left her lips, she regretted it. Where was her filter for God's sake?

Ian raised a sardonic brow. "Oh?"

This was no time for modesty, but she couldn't help feeling utterly exposed in nothing but her blouse and bikini panties. A light blanket was draped over her hip, but her legs were bare to his gaze from thigh to ankle. He kept a blank expression, professional as a doctor should, but still...

She gave a shaky laugh. "Wait, that didn't come out right. I meant you're the best physician." She cleared her throat and looked at her thigh. "Is the cut very deep? How bad is it?"

"It's not deep at all. You're lucky your jeans were in the way or it would have been worse." Ian's angular jaw was set in taut lines and his clipped tone spoke volumes.

Natasha lifted her eyes to meet his steady gaze. She was still reeling from his touch and the electrifying moment their eyes had met after so many years. Now the sexy sound of his Scottish burr and his nearness were making her heart pound and her senses buzz. This wouldn't do. Ian's intense gaze wreaked havoc on her composure as she wondered what lurked beneath the stillness.

She shivered inwardly, dropping her gaze to compose herself. He could read her like a book and he wouldn't tolerate any artifice or acting on her part. He knew her too well.

"Are you going to stitch it up?" she asked, finding her voice.

"No. I'll close the wound with tissue glue. It should heal without a scar."

"No scar? Oh good." She heaved a sigh of relief. No stitches and no scar. Now if she could just get him to smile, she'd feel a lot better.

"Be sure to keep the area clean and dry for 24 hours."

"I will. Thanks, I appreciate it." Ian's expression didn't soften when she smiled at him. With a sigh, she stared at the unyielding set of his mouth. The same mouth that had once smiled at her with heart-melting tenderness, had crooned Scottish endearments while making love to her, had kissed her *everywhere* into quivering acquiescence. All of it had been wonderful until seven years ago when she'd broken off their engagement and he'd thundered, *"Stay out of my life!"*

"How did you get cut like that?" he asked, jarring her from her musings.

"I don't know. One minute I was rushing home on my lunch break, and the next I felt a tug on my dance bag. When I pulled back, something sharp sliced across my thigh."

He touched her leg again and she jerked in response.

"Hold still," he said firmly. One masterful hand held her thigh immobile as the other treated the cut. "Are you in pain?"

"A bit."

He slanted a sympathetic look her way. "I'm almost done. I'll give you something for the pain before you leave if you still need it."

Natasha nodded and bit her lip. It wasn't so much the pain that was jolting; his touch was making her heart race and awakening every nerve portal of her body. She closed her eyes and cast aside the thrilling memory of his hands caressing her legs when they'd first made love. *Think of him as a doctor, nothing more.*

When he finished tending the wound, he straightened and folded his arms over his chest. "When was the last time you ate?" His keen eyes bored into hers.

"I had breakfast this morning. Why do you ask?" She drew aside the light blanket to inspect the large bandage wrapped around her thigh

He studied her with thoughtful deliberation. "You passed out earlier and you're thinner than I remember. Have you been on some crazy diet?"

"No, of course not," she said, wincing as she sat up. "It's all the dancing I've been doing." She wasn't about to divulge that Simon had rudely told her, "Better not lose those round tits and ass, babe. The role calls for it."

Ian's dark brows furrowed. "You used to love food." His elegant surgeon's hand turned her face toward him and his eyes settled on hers with the familiarity born of intimacy. Their eyes locked like lovers, electrified by the memory of their ill-fated passion years ago when his mere touch could set her on fire. The feel of his long fingers gently touching her face made Natasha's heart hurt. His unswerving gaze was fathomless as he stared at her.

"I still do." She drew in a heavy sigh and broke eye contact as she struggled to tether unraveling emotions. Did he remember how amazing it had been between them? Even in his sterile office, and despite the sharp headache budding behind her eyes, Ian aroused turbulent emotions inside her. She felt hot and cold and shaky at once reliving the memory of their heartbreaking split. He'd been her first and only love. No man she'd dated since had filled his shoes...or captured her heart. Especially not the last guy she'd dated. Tony Martin had been the exact opposite of Ian. Try as she might to forget Ian by dating Tony, it hadn't worked—especially when Tony revealed his violent personality. After he unleashed his nasty temper on her, she ended things right away.

Natasha's phone beeped with a text message bringing her back to her present predicament. On the way to Ian's office, between panicking and fighting nausea, she'd texted the stage manager and alerted Elisha that she'd had a minor accident and would be late.

"Will I be able to dance tomorrow?" she asked, fighting the urge to check the text.

"No. Not for several days."

"Several days?" Her shoulders slumped in spite of her resolve to be strong.

He frowned. "Do you want the wound to open again?"

"No, but..." How could she tell him this show was crucial to her career, when it was her career that had been the catalyst of their break-up?

"Follow my directions and you'll be as good as new. When was your last tetanus shot?"

Natasha shrugged. "A long time ago. Just before summer camp." A vision of Simon's snarling face suddenly made her frantic to leave. She swung her legs over the side. "I have to get back to rehearsal."

"You're not leaving until you get a tetanus shot. And you're not going to rehearsal today." Ian's steely eyes brooked no arguments. He was annoyingly authoritarian, yet a brilliant physician and a born healer. She had a scrapbook filled with newspaper and magazine articles about Dr. Ian MacGregor, the eminent laser surgeon and dermatologist, who worked magic removing disfiguring scars and birthmarks. His recent laser invention had catapulted him into celebrity status and garnered him billions.

But it was his work with underprivileged children and adults that made Natasha's heart swell with pride. Since she'd last seen him, he had traveled extensively with Doctors Without Borders and The Smile Train, removing the stigma of disfiguring cleft palates and port wine birthmarks for those who couldn't afford it. Ian would insist on not letting her leave until he could "fix" whatever was wrong with her, but she couldn't stay a moment longer.

"I don't want a shot. I have to leave now!" Not going to rehearsal was out of the question.

Ian's silver-green eyes darkened to gun metal grey as they zeroed in on her with such ferocity she fought the urge to squirm. "What in bloody hell is going on, Tasha?"

She lifted her chin. "I'm starring in a new show and we start previews tomorrow. If I don't get back to dress rehearsal, I'm going to get fined, and possibly replaced."

Ian's lip curled as he shook his head. "Nothing has changed. The show must go on. Comes before everything. Right, Tasha?"

His ironic tone irked the hell out of her. "Yes, that's right. Just like your patients always come first," she retorted. His accusation rubbed a raw spot as they faced an impasse. He was right. Nothing had changed—he was as stubborn and narrow-minded as ever when it came to her.

Natasha inched toward the edge, ready to get off the table, when his hand clamped down on her shoulder.

"Don't get up. Tetanus shot first," he said, turning to the table beside her.

She twisted her neck to see if the syringe was there, but she couldn't see over his broad shoulders. "Fine, I'll take the shot. In my arm and from someone other than you."

"I wasn't planning on it," he said coolly. "Judy will be in shortly." He turned and stalked away.

Natasha got off the examining table when he shut the door. She promptly called her agent, Marty Cranshaw, only to get the bad news that Simon had replaced her temporarily and called a put-in rehearsal for Lisette.

"No sense in going to the theatre now. Most likely they'll be there all night. Go home and rest, hon," Marty said in a caring voice.

"I will, but make no mistake, Marty. I'll be back on that stage stronger than ever for opening night," she said fervently.

Marty chuckled. "I know you will. Have I ever doubted you?"

"Nope, and that's why I love you. Bye, Marty," Natasha said, hanging up with a smile.

A smiling, middle-aged woman walked in holding a pair of blue scrubs in one hand and a small metal tray with a syringe in the other hand. "I brought these pants for you to put on after I give you the shot. We keep a few extra pairs in the office for the nurses."

"Thanks. That's very kind of you. I can't exactly leave here in a leather jacket and panties," Natasha said grimacing. "Which arm do you want? Right or left?"

"Neither. Doc ordered it in your gluteus muscle. Bottoms up," Judy said cheerfully.

"Great." Natasha rolled her eyes and privately cursed Ian. "Let's get it over with then."

"First a tiny jab, then a bit of stinging as the liquid goes in. Relax your muscles so it won't hurt," Nurse Judy said. She pulled on plastic gloves and lowered the edge of Natasha's panties, rubbing alcohol on the spot she'd inject.

Natasha gritted her teeth and silently endured the needle even though it hurt when the liquid went in.

"Okay, we're finished, dear. If the area gets sore or swollen, put an ice pack or a bag of frozen veggies on it. That should take care of it," Judy said reassuringly.

With a nod, Natasha turned over and reached for the scrubs.

"I love your hair color. I want to dye mine the same shade of red, but yours looks natural," Judy said, patting her short curly brown hair.

"It is." Natasha smiled. "You should go for it. It would look great on you."

Judy grinned broadly. "Thanks, I think I will. You're the Broadway actress aren't you?" she asked as she helped Natasha into the drawstring pants.

"Yes. Do you like musicals?"

Judy's big brown eyes sparkled with enthusiasm. "I *love* musicals. They're my biggest indulgence. I heard you're starring in 'The Bee's Knees'. When is it—"

A few sharp raps on the door interrupted her question as Ian entered. "All done?"

"Yes. All done, doc." Judy winked at Natasha and left the room.

"Are you planning any more surprise jabs before you let me go?" Natasha inquired with a sleek lift of one brow.

Ian's lips twitched. "You needed the shot, so don't complain. You can leave now, but you'll have a hard time finding a taxi at this hour. My car service will take you home."

"Thanks, that's kind of you," she said, grateful for his consideration.

"Are you still in pain?"

Natasha gave a half-shrug. "Not too much. I'll take a painkiller when I get home if it feels worse."

He handed her two prescriptions and written instructions. "Come back in a week for a recheck. I'm leaving for London tomorrow. Carla will give you an appointment with my partner, Dr. Delacorte."

Natasha hid her disappointment. He didn't intend to see her again? Ian was acting so detached, it made her nostalgic for the Ian of before—the young man who'd told her she was his first love, his only love. If he hadn't been so dead set on making her leave everything behind to join him in Scotland, things would have worked out between them. It was ironic he was still in town. *All that time wasted apart.* He had been too damn proud and stubborn to take her calls afterward, making her withdraw and immerse herself full force in her career to heal the pain of their split.

"Tell me something," she said, cn impulse. "Why are you still living in New York when you were so eager to make Scotland your permanent home?"

A flash of annoyance hardened his features. "I intend to move back as soon as my clinic is ready. It's taken longer than I'd planned," he said in a strained voice.

"Oh. I'm sorry to hear it," she said softly. Natasha recalled his Aunt Maggie, whom she'd stayed in touch with over the years, telling her that Ian's inheritance was still unresolved. Was it because of that? *Better not go there.* The shuttered look on Ian's face silenced further questions.

Ian's eyes narrowed on Natasha. She might sound concerned and have a kind heart, but there was no room in it for him. Her fair cheeks glowed pink and her wide blue eyes were clouded with disappointment, yet he felt no compunction to feed her curiosity. Not now, especially when reclaiming Glenhaven was so close at hand.

The first time he'd set eyes on Natasha was when she'd visited from the States with her parents. She was a dreamy-eyed dazzler, recently graduated from Juilliard and ripe for romance. Ian's father, Malcolm, and her father, Walter, had known each cther since they were students at Oxford, but it was the first time Ian had met Natasha. From that moment on he couldn't get enough of her. Her warmth and sparkling wit were just what he'd needed during the lowest point of his life when he'd learned many disturbing things about his late father. Drawn into the cocoon of her beautiful heart, Ian had immediately set out to keep her in Scotland as long as he could and make her fall in love with him as rapidly, and completely, as he had with her.

She'd stayed the whole summer and captivated not only Ian, but also his Aunt Maggie and Uncle Ranald, the caretakers of Glenhaven Estate. Tasha had embraced Scotland as if she'd always lived there. He had loved sharing his homeland with her and she'd been as delighted as a kid at Disneyworld. She'd wanted to explore every castle, sample the local food and fine Scottish whiskey and meet his friends and neighbors. By the end of that glorious summer, he wanted to keep her with him forever, but they embarked on a long-distance romance for two long years, taking numerous passion-filled trips back and forth while she performed in America and he finished his doctoral degree in biomedical science. The moment he graduated, he proposed and she accepted, tears of joy flowing down her cheeks.

Sharp desire made him shift his stance as he stared at Tasha, a stunning woman now. More enticing than ever.

"If anyone can solve this, it's you, Dr. Who," Natasha said, jolting him back to the present.

Ian stiffened at hearing her nickname for him and the teasing intonation in her voice.

"Don't you remember I used to call you that?" she said, a soft smile playing at her rosy lips.

"No," he lied, looking away from her tempting mouth. Of course, he remembered. Tasha had loved the popular British sci fi show since she'd first seen it.

"I think you do." The tiny dimple at the left corner of her mouth deepened seductively. It was the same dimple that had lured him to kiss her for the first time. Ian's palms grew damp while he scrutinized Natasha's face. *Still the face of an angel—a wayward one.* Her creamy complexion, flushed pink now, was framed by long, burnished copper curls. Luminous, curly-lashed blue eyes tantalized him, and her mouth, lush and pink, held his attention. It was the sweetest mouth he'd ever kissed—and the most deceptive. *I want a chance to make it on Broadway. Theatre is my life. I love you, Ian, but I would be miserable without performing.* She'd said those words when she'd broken off their engagement—after telling him for months that she loved him and couldn't wait to be his wife! He had offered his love and a wonderful life complete with a castle and servants in Scotland, but she had made an immediate about-face right after her controlling mother had interfered.

Anitra had flown to Glenhaven from New York the previous day to muck things up between them. He recalled their meeting as if it were yesterday. The witch had laughed mockingly in his face as she'd spewed hateful words. *Natasha needs to spread her wings. She's destined to be a Broadway star like me. You didn't really think she'd give up her career to marry you and move to Scotland, did you? To be a country doctor's wife surrounded by sheep? My daughter adores the theatre, much more than she'll ever love you!*

Ian had barely held onto his temper and hadn't given into the urge to drag Anitra's bony behind out of his castle for good. Unfortunately, her harsh words were confirmed the next day when Natasha ended their engagement—by phone. He'd never forget the feeling of being gutted by her and he wasn't about to waste another second trying to figure her out. Impatient to end their little visit, Ian took hold of her elbow and helped her down from the table.

"Does your mother know you're injured?" he asked curtly.

"No, and I plan to keep it that way. I'm not the same girl you knew seven years ago. I've made it on my own, *without* Anitra's help."

"Still not calling her mum?" he said with a shake of his head.

"Nope. As far as Anitra's concerned, she's too young to have a thirty year old daughter," Natasha said ironically.

Ian snorted. "So that's how it is. Pity that."

"I don't want to talk about Anitra. Can't we make peace, Ian? Or are you going to continue scowling at me?"

Natasha's gaze was direct as she waited for his answer. Now that she'd brought it into the open, he couldn't summon the initial bitterness he'd felt at seeing her again. He just felt empty inside. She had once held the deepest part of his heart and soul captive and he'd loved her ardently, but they had no future together.

Ian headed toward the door and said, "Time to go, wee *nyaff.*"

"Just a minute." Natasha grabbed his sleeve and faced him with fiery blue eyes as she tossed her flaming curls. "Don't call me an irritating little person!" She thrust her chin up and smiled slyly. "*Dunderheid,*" she retaliated, daring to insult him.

Ian stifled the rumble of caustic laughter rising in his chest. They hadn't spent more than an hour together and they were already trading insults. Tasha had a way of getting under his skin and provoking him more than anyone else could, yet her quick wit never ceased to entertain him.

Striding out the door, he squashed the powerful urge to turn and grab the maddening redhead and kiss her senseless. And that wasn't all he felt like doing.

SOPHIA KNIGHTLY - BIO

USA Today bestselling author, Sophia Knightly, loves to cook up hot romance and delicious humor in her feel-good stories. Whether it's romantic suspense, romantic comedy or chick lit, her books are fun and sexy contemporary romances that feature hot alpha heroes and strong, smart women.

A two-time Maggie award finalist and a P&E Readers' Poll finalist, she is traditionally published by St. Martin's Press, Kensington and Samhain Publishing. Her popular Tropical Heat Series books, *Wild for You* and *Sold on You*, have consistently been on multiple Amazon bestselling lists and sold over 100,000 copies.

When not writing or reading, she loves walking the beach, exploring museums, going to the theatre, enjoying good food, and watching movies. One of her favorite pastimes remains simply watching people, especially those in love!

Sign up for her "new release" newsletter at:
http://SophiaKnightly.net/newsletter-sign-up.html
Write to her at: SophiaKnightly@gmail.com
Follow her on Twitter @SophiaKnightly
"Like" her Facebook author page at:
http://on.fb.me/vGfJ5t
Visit her website at: www.SophiaKnightly.net

WILD FOR YOU Book Trailer:
http://youtu.be/XtVlFBdaHvs

SOLD ON YOU Book Trailer:
http://youtu.be/X20NbJElrvM

GRILL ME, BABY Book Trailer:
http://youtu.be/6Y07iUPt3rg

LOOK FOR THESE BOOKS BY SOPHIA KNIGHTLY

HEART MELTER (Heartthrob Series, Book Two) precedes HEART TAMER

When dazzling Broadway star Natasha White lands in Dr. Ian MacGregor's office wounded, the healer in him can't turn his ex-fiancée away. Still bitter over their break-up, Ian tries to deny the combustible attraction that re-ignites as he becomes her fierce protector.

Natasha White has no idea why anyone would knife her on a crowded street in Times Square. At first she thinks the cut on her thigh is an accident, but as frightening events unravel, she learns the mob is after an incriminating flash drive they think she has.

After their break-up years ago, Natasha never stopped loving Ian and when he whisks her away to his Highland castle, their hot chemistry consumes them as they dodge impending danger. Ian will do anything to guard Natasha, but will their love be strong enough to survive the shocking secrets revealed?

*   *   *

HEART RAIDER (Heartthrob Series, Book One)
by Sophia Knightly

Stranded together during a rampaging hurricane...

Hot passion explodes between a reclusive billionaire and
a headstrong reporter seeking his exclusive story...a
story that could get her killed.

Hunted by someone desperate to silence her...

Daredevil TV reporter Veronique "Ronnie" Whitcomb is
charismatic, fun-loving, and loyal to a fault. Especially to
the man she fell in love with fifteen years ago. He's now a
self-made billionaire, and at the center of a public scandal
so hot and juicy, Ronnie must get an exclusive
interview...an interview that will vindicate him and

expose the real criminal behind the scintillating headlines. Her life is in jeopardy, but her love for Nick might cause the real danger.

He'll risk his life - and his heart - to keep her alive...

Financial whiz, Nick Cameron rose from an underprivileged life to become one of America's youngest corporate billionaires. Now he's laying low on a barrier island, far away from the raging media storm that nearly destroyed him. When little Ronnie Whitcomb shows up on his doorstep, all grown up and heart-stoppingly beautiful, he tries to deny his feelings for her, but a hurricane strands them on the island together. Keeping Ronnie at arm's length becomes impossible.

*   *   *

WILD FOR YOU
(Tropical Heat Series, Book One)

To Love, Honor and Protect

Detective Clay Blackthorne has his hands full when he promises to safeguard an old college pal's sister without letting her know what he's up to. He never imagines that lively Marisol Calderon will knock his socks off and put a ring on his finger--and all at his suggestion! Their marriage of convenience is meant to protect her and Clay doesn't plan on being hitched for long to the tempting beauty. But the honeymoon sure feels real to him...

Sassy Marisol is used to doing whatever she wants--and right now her plan is to shake up the hot detective's hard-edged demeanor. But the fun turns to danger when a mystery stalker bent on marrying her marks her as his prey. Temporarily becoming Clay's wife seems like a practical way to thwart the stalker. But as passion ignites and Marisol falls for the tender heart buried beneath the tough detective's chest, Clay's true identity is revealed and she begins to wonder who--if anyone--she can trust...

*   *   *

SOLD ON YOU
(Tropical Heat Series, Book Two)

Just Say Yes!

Confirmed bachelor Dr. Marcos Calderon is in hot water. He needs to come up with a fake fiancée fast or he'll disappoint his beloved grandma who's arriving on the next flight to meet her. Proper social worker Gabriela Morales should fit the bill--but tonight, in that sexy, slit-to-there red evening gown, she looks anything but proper.

Gabriela only volunteered for the hospital's charity bachelorette auction to benefit a cause dear to her heart. Now she's reeling from the hot doctor's bid of fifteen thousand dollars for a weekend date with her! She's not sure what Dr. Handsome has in mind, but the smoldering look in his eyes is unmistakable...

*   *   *

GRILL ME, BABY

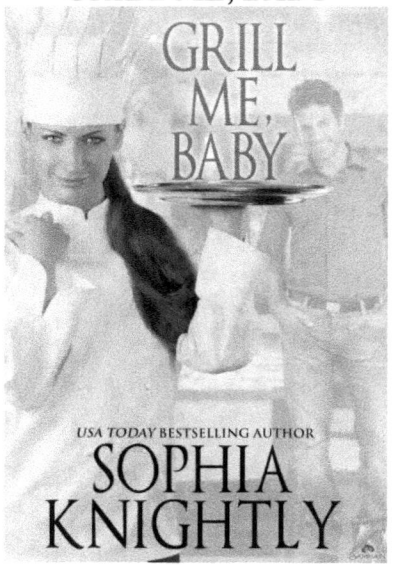

The heat is on...

Raised among women who taught him to cook at his family's Buenos Aires restaurant, master chef Paolo Santos deftly works his culinary wiles--and his gypsy charm--on posh Flamingo Island's female clientele.

The tastiest tidbit on the island, though, is cool, elegant Michaela Willoughby. The redhead's slender curves are as enticing as her rabbit-food menus are maddening. And she's his main competition for the chance of a lifetime.

Michaela overcame her own weight issues to become Flamingo Island's premiere spa chef. Now she has a chance to share her innovative recipes for healthy living on a new cooking show--if she can somehow outshine

Paolo. His sizzling, Latin-lover looks are more heart stopping than his decadent cooking. And she'd love nothing better than to stick a fork in his outsized ego.

When the stage lights ignite, so does the competition...and a sexual chemistry no one--least of all Paolo and Michaela--saw coming. Suddenly, separating business from pleasure is as impossible as separating a scrambled egg. And the big question isn't whose knife cuts fastest...it's whose heart can take the most heat.

Warning: Contains two hot chefs duking it out in a lively showdown of sexy rivalry. Mix in family drama, luscious recipes and spicy mischief, and there's more than just steam rising out of the kitchen. May cause lusty cravings for midnight indulgences.

* * *

PAGING DR. HOT

A love prescription so potent only the hottest doctor can fill it.

Miami TV reporter Francesca Lake is on a manhunt…or rather, a doctor hunt. Frankie wasn't always a hypochondriac. Her motto used to be "Fear is not an option", but everything changed with her mom's near-fatal heart attack. Now a day doesn't go by where she isn't worried about something.

After a harrowing incident in the hospital ER, she has a life-altering epiphany. She needs to find a marriage-minded doctor ASAP—one who will calm her fears so she can get on with her life.

So begins a series of amorous escapades and startling revelations as she works her way through the list of eligibles: an outrageous Aussie sex therapist, a brilliant neurosurgeon (who's wired the wrong way), and a handsome Cuban cardiologist.

None of them compares to hunky Dr. Harrison Taylor...but there's a problem. Much as Harrison's rugged physique, forest-green eyes and warm smile make her senses wobbly, she needs a people doctor, not the vet for her miniature dachshund Romeo. Besides, Harrison's propensity for crazy stunts would only make her worry more.

Frankie is trying to be sensible, but her heart and her outspoken dog are conspiring against her...

Warning: Contains juicy secrets and romantic misadventures between a loveable hypochondriac and three hot doctors. Side effects may include intense yearnings for a strong doctor, an adorable miniature dachshund, and an impromptu trip to sultry Miami.

* * *

TROPICAL HEAT SERIES BOX SET

Two fun, sexy and heartwarming romances of Sophia Knightly's Tropical Heat Series in one bundled volume.

In *Wild for You* (Book One), Detective Clay Blackthorne has his hands full when he promises to safeguard an old college pal's sister without letting her know what he's up to. He never imagines that lively Marisol Calderon will knock his socks off and put a ring on his finger--and all at his suggestion! Their marriage of convenience is meant to protect her and Clay doesn't plan on being hitched for long to the tempting beauty. But the honeymoon sure feels real to him...

Sassy Marisol is used to doing whatever she wants--and right now her plan is to shake up the hot detective's hard-edged demeanor. But the fun turns to danger when a mystery stalker bent on marrying her marks her as his prey. Temporarily becoming Clay's wife seems like a practical way to thwart the stalker. But as passion ignites and Marisol falls for the tender heart buried beneath the tough detective's chest, Clay's true identity is revealed and she begins to wonder who--if anyone--she can trust...

In *Sold on You,* (Book Two) Confirmed bachelor Dr. Marcos Calderon is in hot water. He needs to come up with a fake fiancée fast or he'll disappoint his beloved grandma who's arriving on the next flight to meet her. Proper social worker Gabriela Morales should fit the bill--but tonight, in that sexy, slit-to-there red evening gown, she looks anything but proper.

Gabriela only volunteered for the hospital's charity bachelorette auction to benefit a cause dear to her heart. Now she's reeling from the hot doctor's bid of fifteen thousand dollars for a weekend date with her! She's not sure what Dr. Handsome has in mind, but the smoldering look in his eyes is unmistakable...